The Ghost in Mr. Pepper's Bed

by
Sigrid Vansandt

ISBN:
ISBN-13: 978-1980741381

CONTENTS

To all my wonderful readers. Thank you so much for your kind emails, your sense of adventure and your willingness to read my crazy books! I truly hope they bring you pleasure, happy moments, and sweet dreams.

Sigrid

Chapter 1

A soft moonlight filtered in across the sleeping elderly man's bald head and illuminated the room in a muted silvery radiance. The camper's small window directly above his feet was slightly opened to allow the cool May night air into the tiny sleeping chamber. Outside, the insect population was in its second movement of the evening's musical concerto and the man's breathing seemed to wax and wane with the gentle rhythms of their songs.

Mr. Pepper, as he was known to the residents of The Whispering Pines RV Park, was a tidy person and the camper he called home, was, in all ways, a reflection of his domestic philosophy. The tiny bedroom in which he slept was sparsely decorated but with a masculine penchant for quiet colors and utilitarian necessities. There was a flashlight within easy reach of his bed, a revolver tucked into the bookshelf next to the Farmer's Almanac and a dusty bottle of brandy for cold nights hidden in the bottom drawer of the bedside cabinet.

His bedroom boasted of one sentimental item, and it hung on the wall next to the open window right above Mr. Pepper's feet. It was a photograph in a slim metal frame housing a picture of a young, attractive woman sporting a 1960s bouffant hairdo. Like a guardian angel, she beamed a cheerful smile from her home on the camper wall. Tonight, the sleeping Mr. Pepper peacefully dreamed of the pretty girl, Eloise, his wife of forty-five years who was now deceased.

A cool wind whipped up outside the camper and twirled its way like a zephyr through the open bedroom window into the tiny room. It moaned softly and hung in a fog directly above the lightly snoring Pepper. With a joyful sigh, the mist settled itself as closely as possible against the warm, sleeping elderly man.

Nothing and no one stirred the peace. Somewhere, though, in the recesses of Mr. Pepper's subconscious, something sent up little question marks to his slumbering mind causing him to shift uneasily in his cozy nest of blankets and pillows. The chilly, misty bedmate lying beside him readjusted itself as well, and that's when poor Pepper found himself uncomfortably awake.

At first, he thought he'd been dreaming of his wife, but as he pulled himself into an upright position in his bed, he realized something was amiss. He focused his eyes on the photo of Eloise to bring himself into the conscious present and it was at that moment Eloise Pepper's framed photo rattled ominously against the paneling. At first, subtle tremors took hold of the camper as if it was being buffeted by a strong wind. But soon the shaking picked up and increased its energy until it crescendoed with a series of violent vertical and horizontal jerks.

Mr. Pepper was being tossed around inside the camper like a lottery ball at a Saturday night bingo parlor. Trying frantically to remember what one should do in an earthquake, he found his groggy mind lacking, but as he rolled once more from one side of his bed to the other, that same brain quickly reminded him there hadn't been an earthquake in Missouri in over a hundred years.

As the rocking escalated, Mr. Pepper grabbed desperately to the edges of his mattress for stability. His befuddled brain tried to make sense of the bucking-bronco movements of his camper. Like Aladdin riding his magic carpet, poor Mr. Pepper also felt the effects of air turbulence. Queasiness was taking hold, so he held on for dear life, becoming aware of a mist rising beside him on the bed and encircling him within a tornado-type cone.

A woman's sleepy sigh followed by a whimpering sound made Mr. Pepper's blood almost come to a crashing halt in his veins. Rapidly blinking his eyelids, the pajama-wearing septuagenarian tried to make sense of what he was seeing. It was when Eloise's photograph lifted off its hook and levitated in mid-air for a few uncomfortable seconds, that Mr. Pepper realized his situation was far outside any rational attempts at an explanation.

It was a good thing he quit trying to understand because what was truly needed in his situation was excellent reflexes. His dearly departed wife's photo took flight right at his head as he ducked. It slammed into the opposite wall barely missing Pepper's balding pate. That's when all hell broke loose inside the camper. Screeching and guttural sounds reminiscent of cats fighting exploded like a mini-bomb in the six-foot by four-foot room.

With the camper rocking as if a wind was buffeting it from all directions, Mr. Pepper scrambled off the bed while things were knocked about and blankets were sucked up into the air and flung into corners. He stumbled out into the kitchen area and frantically tried to find the front door latch to escape the whirlwind of flying objects, yelling female voices, and the occasional tug on his person from unseen, cold hands.

Once out into the darkness of the night, he turned to watch the cyclonic activity whipping around inside his aluminum home. With both hands, he pulled on the gray tufts of hair encircling the sides and back of his otherwise bald cranium and shook his head in disbelief at the sight. Was he being fought over by two unseen women? He quickly realized the storm wasn't abating inside, so he gingerly made his way in bare feet over to Marnie's, the park's owner. Marnie would know what to do.

Behind him and inside his camper, a gun went off, making Mr. Pepper jump and hunch up as if he expected the bullet to be about to make an impact on his backside at any second. Feeling no sting, he gave up worrying about his tender toes and toddled down the perfectly manicured gravel drive. Not stopping once, he made it to Marnie Scott's door yelling, "Let me in, Marnie! I think my wife is trying to kill me!"

Chapter 2

"You'd better not eat that, Willard. Your digestion isn't what it used to be," Sonya Caruthers explained to her five-pound, tan terrier who came popping through the doggy door from the backyard. In his mouth was an old plastic chew bone he'd probably buried months ago and had dug up sometime in the last hour. "Last week you ate the fringe off my grandmother's old woolen blanket. Your stomach made the most terrible sounds for two days. Don't let plastic be the reason for your next visit to the vet."

Willard's button-sized coal-black eyes blinked as an acknowledgment to her comment while his mouth smiled around the dirt encrusted orange bone. If a passing neighbor or even a newly arrived bird to one of the taller bushes hugging Sonya's house had peeked in at that moment, they would have wondered if Mrs. Sonya Caruthers was perhaps a bit dingy or touched in the head.

Who talks to animals? They might be thinking or maybe, what an odd assortment of clothing for a woman to be wearing!

Dressed in a royal blue tunic, a long, floral scarf flung about her neck and tie-dyed colored tights, coupled with orange zippered high-heeled ankle boots, Sonya C. cut a unique fashion figure. Her kinky brown hair, knobby jewelry, and green eyes were on the large side, while her feet, lavender-lipsticked mouth, and Victorian cottage were definitely on the small.

Since the age of seven, she'd been comfortable picking up the inner feelings of most people and domesticated animals, as well as with having the occasional conversation with a stranded being known to the rest of us as a ghost. By fourteen, Sonya was adept at keeping her talent quiet, and by twenty-five, she'd accepted her gifts and progressed to using them to help anyone or anything that needed her. At forty, she was an early widow and had decided to present her spiritual therapy services to the community by running a nice business from her home.

People stopped by to seek out her help. Sometimes it might be a newbie ghost requesting Sonya's help in accepting their new life or the exact opposite, one of the living wishing dead Uncle Harry would cross over and leave them in peace.

Picking up Willard, her pint-sized terrier, with a gentleness and respect most people don't bother showing to their human loved ones, Sonya brushed him free of his backyard dirt and deposited her furry friend of five years onto his favorite perch. She held out her hand for the bone because Willard, once committed to lavishing his attentions on a chew toy of any kind, would most likely gnaw on it until he'd consumed it entirely. Plastic isn't the friend of dogs, and where he'd found this toy was anyone's guess.

Slightly lowering his eyelids, Willard resisted giving up the chew bone. He rolled over to show his adorable belly and waved one front paw as a salute to his honest intentions. Sonya laughed at his antics, scratched the presented tummy and shook her head. Willy was a con, but a charming one. She sighed and said, "Don't whine to me when your stomach hurts later, and you're sleeping in the guest room tonight. Understand?"

Flipping himself over, he performed a deep stretch and a couple of quick circles. He worked himself down on top of his bone in a curled up ball and shut his eyes for his mid-day nap. Sonya waited for the snoring to begin. Once he was asleep, she retrieved a rawhide bone from the cupboard and made the switch with Willy making one sleepy snort for her troubles. When he awoke, he'd be perfectly happy with the substitute and his inside plumbing could continue to operate peacefully.

Moving quietly, so as not to wake him, Sonya turned to the one domestic chore she enjoyed the most--watering her flowers in the front garden. The rather diminutive Victorian cottage of Sonya and Willard nestled comfortably between a nineteen-thirties Tudor and a magnificent Dutch Colonial. Sonya's home was extremely well-maintained. It was painted a happy color of canary yellow with white trim and a wrap-around porch. Festooned with flowers at every window and along the brick front walk, it graced Pickwick Street with a nostalgic nod to those finer aesthetic sentiments appreciated by our more genteel ancestors at the end of the nineteenth century.

She'd made her home in Willow Valley and had lived contentedly there for over five years. A widow, she came to the quaint southern Missouri town after her husband, Bud, passed away and set up shop doing what she'd always done, assisting souls on either side of the great divide. A few Willow Valley eyebrows were raised at the shingle she hung outside her house, *Ghost Therapist* but owing to the new tenant's excellent gardening abilities and responsible maintenance of one of Willow Valley's prettiest historic homes, most of its citizens chalked up her profession to eccentricity or talent. Either way, they concluded, she was an excellent addition to the neighborhood.

As she picked up the watering can still sitting on her kitchen counter, a chilly breeze floated by her. Sonya's extra-sensory perception told her she wasn't alone. Willard, awakened by the presence, growled in a low tone and hopped down from his spot. His nails and paws made clicking sounds as he sped into the kitchen and barked and bounced in a dance directly under the kitchen table. Sonya shook her head.

"I think we have a visitor, Willard. There's only one person who prefers perching on furniture instead of sitting on chairs. You shouldn't be so rude every time he visits," she chastised him gently.

Out of nowhere, a red ball dropped from the middle of the kitchen table and bounced across the kitchen floor out into the living room with Willard in hot pursuit.

"Go chase that, you wee mongrel!" boomed a man's voice thick with a Scottish brogue. "How are you, my love? Miss me?"

Chapter 3

"Fritz, back so soon?" Sonya asked as she finished filling the watering can at the sink. Fritz was short for Fitswilliam. He was also known, in more genteel circles, as Lord Fitswilliam Dunbar, a Scottish Laird, who died from a fever after a day of shooting grouse.

Sonya called him Fritz instead of Fits because, as she put it, she wasn't always going to the trouble to use his full name, and Fitz sounded rude. He had lived a full life two hundred years ago on his ancestral estate in the Highlands of Scotland. And these days, now that he was dead, he still maintained a busy existence helping Sonya, annoying his dead wife, Mary, and toying with the unsuspecting living, mainly the next-door neighbor, Mrs. Townsend.

Fritz, for that matter, would have answered to Chuckles if Sonya's taste ran in that direction because he was completely smitten with her in every way. His lack of a corporeal body in no way hindered his fervent love for Sonya. After his death in 1815, he'd taken to traveling the world and as most ghosts do, he lost his concept of time. It wasn't until he'd been enjoying himself in a posh grand hotel in Montreal, Canada, as a resident specter for a few years that he was reminded one evening how many decades had actually passed since his death. It was the night that he laid eyes on Sonya that changed his afterlife forever.

She'd come to attend a convention of paranormal studies, and he'd spied her from his favorite position for people-watching perched on the top of a Steinway piano in the main entrance hall. Sonya was a colorful dresser by any standard, but it was her sunny personality, beautiful eyes and way of smiling at people with true friendliness that entranced Fritz. Her warmth and genuine goodness intoxicated him.

He'd floated and hovered around her the entire weekend until finally, one evening as she was letting herself into her room and he was peeking at her from the hallway's massive crystal chandelier, Sonya said, "Would you like to come in and have a nice chat?"

Fritz noted the lack of living people in the hall and wondered if the bright-eyed woman was slightly touched in the head. She turned and looked straight up at him.

"I'm talking to you, there in the chandelier. You've been following me now for two days. Would you like to come in for a talk? We might as well get to know each other."

Fritz was stunned. It was the first time since his death that anyone had actually talked to him like he was a person other than the ghosts he kept company with occasionally. Granted, she did point out his location in the ceiling's lighting fixture, but, for all intents and purposes, she didn't appear discombobulated by the situation. As a gentleman, he hesitated to accept an invitation from a woman to visit her bedroom.

He cleared his throat for he wanted to make a good

impression and said, "Why, thank you, but it might appear unseemly for a gentleman to call on you without a chaperon."

"I hardly need a chaperone at my age and it's the twenty-first century," Sonya replied. "It would be much easier on my neck if you popped down here to my level."

"Twenty-first century?" Fritz mumbled. There it was. He was utterly shocked by his loss of worldly time.

"Yes, I can tell by your dress and your manner, you are most likely from the early nineteenth century. Now, I must go inside because if someone sees me talking to the ceiling here in the hall, they may call the closest sanitarium to deploy their pick-up team to collect me."

Fritz saw the wisdom of her comment and answered, "Yes, dear lady, I'll be right down."

They had a lovely talk and Fritz, for the first time in almost two hundred years, found himself feeling more alive than dead and more human than ghost. Since then, he'd stayed close to Sonya and always called her Sunny. Even though Willard didn't show signs of accepting Fritz's presence in the house, the three of them made a nice family. Sonya kept the two males from being too disagreeable with each other and they, in turn, were completely devoted to her in every way.

"Fritz," Sonya was saying from the kitchen sink as she continued to fill her watering can, "I don't like it when you don't materialize when you're in the house. We've talked about this. If I can't see you, I'm likely to walk through you and that gives me the shivers. Play fair."

"Sunny," he said with a charming Scottish brogue to his voice, "I just wanted to bring you a surprise, but that horse's back end of a dog always ruins the moment."

A butterfly lit on the window seal of the kitchen window. The afternoon sunbeams illuminated the iridescent gold decorating its slender, blue, filigree wings. It stayed perfectly still as if waiting.

"Put your finger out, Sunny," Fritz asked gently. Sonya complied and the fairy-like insect climbed aboard. For a moment, the room was quiet except for the soft ticking of the old grandmother clock in the hall. All too soon, the fragile creature pumped its wings and fluttered out again into the sunlight and the well-tended flower garden.

"Was that you're doing, Fritz, dear?" Sonya asked sweetly.

"It isn't easy getting your point across to our purer dwellers here on Earth," he answered, "but butterflies have a special rapport when it comes to love."

"You're a ghost, my dear, Fritz. I think a spirit might have the advantage over a living human."

Fritz, with a nod to her opinion, said, "Perhaps, but let's not quibble. Did you enjoy my token of affection?"

"It was exquisite, Fritz. Your presents are always… sublime."

Puffed up by Sonya's sweet words, Fritz stretched out contentedly across the table and hummed an old Scottish ballad about star-crossed lovers.

Willard trotted back in and growled at the table. One tiny canine tooth revealed itself as the side of his muzzle lifted slightly. He planted his two front paws on the back of a chair and barked ferociously.

"Here, give him a treat, Fritz." Sonya laid an appropriately sized dog treat on the table next to the materialized Laird of Dunbar. She watched as a wicked grin creased his mouth and he flicked the round meatball across the table with his finger. It took flight and flew like the ball had done earlier out of the room and into the living room. Willard followed it like a heat-seeking missile.

At the same instant, the telephone rang and Sonya grabbed the receiver.

"Hello? Sonya Caruthers speaking."

A worried woman's voice came through clearly. "Sonya, it's Marnie. Do you have some time today for a visit?"

"Sure. Is something wrong?" Sonya asked.

"Early this morning one of my tenants was attacked in his camper. There was a   terrible ruckus and even a weapon fired."

"Umm, maybe you need the police, Marnie."

"I'm not sure. You see at about five o'clock this morning, Mr. Pepper in lot five was sleeping soundly, having a nice dream of being spooned by his wife."

"Well, that doesn't sound so bad."

"Yes and no. His wife's been dead for ten years. When he turned over, he nearly died of fright!"

"Was it her?" Sonya asked.

"He says so. But I never would have believed him until

I saw his camper ablaze with lights, women screaming, and the camper rocking like it was caught in a tornado. We had only a gentle breeze last night."

"You may have something going on other than a ghost issue. Is now a good time for me to come over?"

"Please do."

"I'm on my way." Sonya hung up the phone.

Fritz offered an opinion, "Sounds like a banshee, Sunny, terrible creatures to have on your bad side."

"Perhaps," Sonya said, picking up her keys from their hook. "But it sounds like more than one woman to me. They supposedly heard more than one female voice."

"Poor man," Fritz said shaking his head. "Either way, I don't envy him. It's an unlucky man who finds himself betwixt and between two angry women."

Chapter 4

"We'd better get going, boys. Are you up for a spin on the moped?"

Sonya looked around, but Willard was already off in the direction of the garage at the word moped and Fritz was nowhere to be seen. Going through the house to make sure all was tidy and locked up, Sonya picked up her sunglasses, a doll-sized pair of goggles, put three rawhide bones in her big satchel and slung it on her back.

The back door led to an old carriage house situated in the back of her property. It was conveniently located on an alleyway shared by all the houses on her side of the street. Willard waited impatiently at the newly installed garage door.

Sonya knew by the dance he was doing, shifting quickly from one front paw to the other, that he was antsy to get going.

"Let me get the door," she said thinking how the five pounds of fur at her feet could be extremely pushy at times. Once inside, Sonya lifted a wiggling Willard up and put him into a cushioned crate that was strapped to the back of the two-wheeled vehicle. Without fighting her, Willard was fitted with a pair of miniature goggles over his eyes and an aviator cap made of leather.

"You look dashing, Willard. As a reminder, please don't bark at the Dalmatian, who lives at the end of the block. He always chases us down the street and I don't have time to stop today and walk him back home. Got it?"

Willard snorted. He'd become convinced the Dalmatian was the culprit who had nipped off with the tasty ham bone Sonya gave him two Christmases ago. One of Willy's favorite things to do was to ride past the Dalmatian and bark ferociously trying to stir up trouble by foisting insults on the other dog about the supposedly missing bone. The Dalmatian, in response to the verbal accusations, always leaped off its front porch and ran barking behind Sonya's moped trying to catch Willy but never being quite able to make it.

"Willard, keep it pleasant today. I'm going to the RV park and no fussing with Lewis and Clark, Marnie's dogs, either."

Sonya put on her round white helmet, which resembled an egg and tucked her hair in on all sides. She adjusted her sunglasses on her nose and sat down on the moped. At the turn of a key, the engine hummed to life. With a look over her shoulder, she said loudly enough for Willard to hear, "You'll get your treat at Marnie's if you behave yourself with the Dalmatian as we go by."

Sonya slowly guided the moped down the alleyway with Willard looking over the top of his crate through his big-eyed goggles. The wind picked up with their speed and soon they were zipping down Pickwick Street and onto Main Street. Slowly, Fritz materialized on the front handlebars in a sitting position.

"Fritz! You can't be seen riding like that. It will scare people. Besides, it's like looking through fog and it makes seeing difficult."

"Make up your mind, woman. To materialize, or not to materialize, that is the question!"

"Fritz! I can't see around you," Sonya said as the bright red moped swerved and wobbled in the road. Willard barked excitedly at the reappearance of Fritz while bystanders scratched their heads at the vision of a yapping, cap-wearing terrier, a zippy moped-driving lady, and what appeared to be a blobby-foggy substance hovering on her handlebars passing by on the road.

Fortunately, within five minutes, they came to the outskirts of town where they were less conspicuous.

Highway 59 linked Willow Valley to the outside world. The picturesque town was a favorite with tourists most times of the year. It hosted different events to draw people in, such as antique car shows and arts and crafts fairs, but the one event that put the town on the map was Dog Days.

The three-day event was the brainchild of Willow Valley's mayor, Tobias Miller, during the 1980s. People came from all over the Midwest to parade their pooches along the sidewalks, watch dog treat preparation demonstrations by regional chefs, and visit the many vendors lined along Main Street selling everything from canine cowboy-booties to doggy-strollers. The grand finale was a fashion and talent show sponsored by Posh Pups, a high-end organic food company based in St. Louis, where dogs and designers competed to win the coveted Golden

Paw Award.

Willow Valley's fame as a pet-friendly environment meant that most of its businesses catered to the steady flow of animal lovers who visited, shopped, and sometimes camped for short or long stays.

The Whispering Pines RV Park shared this pet-friendly attitude as well. It was an exceptionally nice place to live or stay, depending on its guest's agenda. Charming flagstone pathways, stonework bathing facilities, and a main lodge built of limestone rock gave the park a nostalgic feel. Once Marnie Scott purchased the park, she renovated the outdoor barbecue pavilion and added a fire-pit area with hanging flower baskets.

Sonya pulled up in front of The Pines' office and removed her helmet. A barrage of barking erupted from inside the office. Willard had refrained from his usual antics with the Dalmatian, but at the friendly greeting from Lewis and Clark, Marnie's two beagles, he yapped loudly as a pleasant fellow should when he's excited to see his buddies.

The door to the office opened and two practically identical beagles bounded out toward the white picket fence, which enclosed a yard for Marnie's personal use. There was a huge display of sniffing, scratching, and general canine exuberance at seeing Willard and Sonya. Lewis and Clark were bright boys and whenever someone visited, they usually hoped to receive some form of a treat. With excellent noses, both beagles had already honed in on the savory something hidden somewhere on Sonya's person.

"When you are all three calm, I've got something for you," she said fiddling with something in the pocket of her jacket. With a fierce determination to reign in their natural energy, Lewis and Clark sat down side-by-side and waited, focusing with rapt attention on Sonya's face.

Willard was eyeing Sonya carefully, too. She was excellent at keeping her promises and since he'd restrained himself from one pleasure, he hoped she wouldn't forget about their deal and would reward him with another.

"Here you are." She handed each pooch a nice-sized bone and they all trotted off in totally separate directions to enjoy them without the threat of interlopers. Marnie bustled out and headed to the gate. Letting herself out, she motioned for Sonya to follow her.

"We can talk as we walk," she said giving Sonya a hug. "Better start with Mr. Pepper. He's threatening to leave as soon as possible. I'd like to reassure him with the idea that I'm trying to settle things quickly."

They walked to a corner of the park where thick cedar trees flanked each side of the main entrance. There, sitting in a pleasant alcove of tall trees and bordered by a row of forsythia bushes, was a lovely classic Airstream camper. An elderly man in his seventies sat in a folding chair listening to a radio playing an Elvis tune. He was wearing a baseball cap, Bermuda shorts, a Hawaiian shirt, white sports socks that came up to his knees and his feet shoved into strap sandals. The two women approached with smiles.

"Mr. Pepper, please let me introduce you to Mrs. Caruthers. She's going to help us with our…problem," Marnie said directing the gentleman's attention away from fiddling with the radio dial and toward Sonya, who stood smiling a bit awkwardly.

Mr. Pepper, upon seeing Sonya, hurriedly wiggled himself out of his chair and hustled over to the two ladies. He unconsciously smoothed his hair down and made an attempt at holding in his stomach. With a smile for Sonya, he invited the two women to join him at his seating area in a shady spot under his rolled out awning.

"If you would, Mr. Pepper, please tell me what happened last night," Sonya asked, making herself comfortable in the camp chair she'd been offered.

"Well, it was like any other night. I let my cat, Henrietta, out and turned off the lights. Nothing unusual occurred until early this morning. I awoke from a dream of my wife lying down beside me and curling up next to me like she used to do for forty-some years."

Mr. Pepper blushed but continued. "I was still half asleep, but as my consciousness took over, I realized something was extremely wrong. That's when I turned over and… it was the most terrifying thing I've ever seen. The camper went crazy, jumping around everywhere, and things were being thrown about everywhere. I finally managed to get out of bed and outside. There was screaming like two women were…for lack of a better word, fighting. That's when I heard the gunshot. Up until that point, I wasn't sure if I was dreaming, but that truly settled it and I made for Marnie's camper."

Marnie and Sonya exchanged uncertain glances.

"Sounds like we may have two female ghosts and they're upset about something. Would you mind, Mr.

Pepper, if I went into your camper? They might still be around and I may be able to find out what's going on."

"Of course, please do," Mr. Pepper said in a surprised tone. "I guess you're used to this sort of thing." He stood up and gallantly opened the door of his RV and let Sonya pass.

Once inside, Sonya moved to the back of the well-made camper. Granite countertops, cherry cabinets, and stainless steel appliances made for a lovely environment. Feeling another presence, she immediately knew it wasn't aggressive. In fact, it was rather sweet and timid. Sonya sent out a simple mental push, kind of like ringing the doorbell to the other side and waited. This presence wasn't keen on communicating.

Sitting on one of the benches of the dining table, she continued to put out invitations until she felt the spirit warm to the idea of talking. It was hesitant to come forward, so Sonya said out loud, "It's okay to let me see you. I'm here because Mr. Pepper has had a terrible fright."

"His name is Saul," came a woman's soft voice. "It was his father's way of being funny. Thank goodness, Saul had a good sense of humor, but I guess he had to with a name like Saul Tand Pepper."

A tinkle of laughter made Sonya smile. The voice had a New Jersey accent and there was a dry comedic tone to its timber.

"How do you know Saul?" Sonya asked tentatively. She never assumed in these situations. A person could be haunted by almost anyone. Ghosts could be flakey creatures. They would follow people home who might be eating their favorite ice cream flavor or someone they overheard making a nasty comment about a beloved baseball team.

"Saul is my husband. I've been keeping watch over him for a few days. There's been a weird ghost hanging around here. It's a woman and I ran her off this morning. She won't be back."

"Do you have any idea why she was here?"

"No, I didn't exactly want to have a cup of coffee with her after I tossed the floozy out of here," Eloise said haughtily. Then quickly changing her tone, as if she felt a bit guilty for being so short, she added, "I know she must be lonely and discontented with her situation. She knows she's dead, but she can't pass over."

"What's your Christian name, Mrs. Pepper?" Sonya asked.

"Eloise."

"Why didn't you pass over, Eloise?"

"You're a bit nosey."

"I'm sorry. I didn't even introduce myself. My name is Sonya Caruthers and my friend who owns this RV park wants me to find out who the ghost is and why it's here. It may begin to frighten others, and I thought if I knew who you were, it might help me to understand this spirit better."

"Listen here, dear, that ghost has nothing to do with Saul and me. She's from around here and I've never met her before. We're from New Jersey and I'm buried back there. Saul always promised himself he would travel once he retired. After I passed away, he bought this camper and took to the road."

"Do you want me to tell Saul we talked?"

"Sure and while you are at it, let him know he needs to go back home. Our daughter needs help with the grandchildren. He's fiddled around out here long enough. Casey, our daughter, has three girls and a worthless husband. She needs her father to go back to Canton and kick Jeff, the jerk, in the pants."

"Will do. It's been nice meeting you, Eloise. You didn't answer my question though about passing over."

Eloise sighed. "Our time over there is different from yours in this dimension. We're tied to our lives and our loved ones by threads of love, commitment, mistreatment and even anger. It's like harp strings. One is plucked and we feel the reverberation. Some of us don't answer the call for many reasons, but I go where my family needs me."

"It's been a pleasure, Eloise. Take care and I'll be seeing you." Sonya stood up and Eloise waved and was gone. There weren't any other energies in the camper. Sonya turned to go and heard a familiar yapping coming from outside. She looked out of the window and saw Willard, Lewis, and Clark zipping across the yard with tails straight out and expressions of high spirits on their canine faces. With a smile and a shrug, she let herself out of the camper and into the sunlight.

Chapter 5

"You're a pretty good runner, Willy, and that bone your lady brought us was top-notch. Wanna see something interesting?" Lewis asked.

"Sure. I smell someone cooking chicken, though. Wouldn't it be better to check that out? Never want to pass up the chance of getting chicken," Willard said, looking back and forth between Lewis and Clark.

"He's right, Lewis," Clark added. *"Chicken is being cooked somewhere close by."* Clark's nose wiggled as the aroma of barbecued poultry wafted through the park.

"True, but protecting Marnie is number one and if you look over there," Lewis' nose directed their attention toward the pit, "that thing standing there makes my back itchy."

Willard and Clark gazed at the place Lewis indicated. An energy hovered by the huge open place in the earth where the backhoe was working at moving dirt. All three dogs barked at the intruder, but none of them made any attempt at chasing after it.

"What is it?" Clark asked.

"Looks like the same thing that lives in my house with Sonya and me," Willard said.

"Lives in your house?" Lewis said, sounding a bit thunderstruck and sitting back on his haunches. *"Whatever that thing is, I don't like it."*

"I could tell you stories, boys. Sonya chases after those things all the time and she's adopted one who enjoys nothing better than to torment me."

Lewis and Clark looked around for Marnie. Not seeing her, they made sure they were touching each other along their flanks for a sense of security.

"Should we run it off?" Clark asked Willard.

"I think so. It's giving me that itchy feeling just by looking at it," Lewis said.

"Boys, I'm not sure about that. Sonya gets upset with me if I chase after those things. If she catches me, she'll be disappointed, and I hate that more than anything."

Lewis and Clark shot each other a quick look.

"We know what you mean. That's the worst, but what if we went over and sniffed at it a bit? That wouldn't hurt would it?" Lewis asked.

"It won't smell like anything, but you can feel them like you do people. Some are weak and some are strong. Some think they're funny and puff air at the back of your head when you're sleeping," Willard said as he lay down thinking about Fritz.

"Willy," Lewis said in an authoritative tone, "I'm going over there to check it out. You and Clark stay put."

"I'm coming, too, Lewis," Clark said and the two beagles cantered off noses low to the ground in the

direction of the ghost.

Every canine instinct within Willard needled him to follow. His skin itched with longing to go with the boys and give a good chase. He looked around and not seeing Sonya, he brightened. This ghost was a freebie. It might not even be one that Sonya was interested in, and in that case, it would be wrong to pass up this glorious opportunity. Willard practically leapt from his laying position and ran the remaining distance to where the boys were.

"Come on, guys!" he barked, taking the lead. "Let's get it!"

Willard led the charge with Lewis and Clark as wingmen. The three dogs barked joyfully as the ghost simply floated to the center of the pit. The canine trio stopped dead at the pit's edge whining frustratedly. Finally, Lewis stopped completely and sat back on his haunches. *"That thing is weird."*

"I'm hungry," Clark sighed and lay down beside his brother.

"Oh, boy, there's Sonya," Willard said nervously.

Sonya stood in the doorway of Mr. Pepper's Airstream camper. Marnie and Mr. Pepper were sitting outside in two comfortable camping chairs. They looked up and smiled as she stepped down to the ground.

"Well?" Marnie asked in a hopeful tone.

Sonya smiled and looked at the diminutive man. "Mr. Pepper, your wife, Eloise, would like to let you know she wants you to go home to New Jersey. She feels your daughter, Casey, and your granddaughters need your help."

Mr. Pepper's eyebrows raised two inches on his forehead. "Eloise? You talked with Eloise?"

"Yes, she's concerned about your son-in-law, Jeff. She thinks he needs a kick in the pants."

Mr. Pepper nodded his head up and down. "That must have been Eloise, all right. She always said it like that. "Jeff needs a kick in the pants." I'd better get my camper ready for the road. Sorry, Marnie, but after last night, I don't want to tussle with Eloise. She's likely to put the hurt on me if I don't take Jeff in hand."

Marnie nodded. "Family first, Mr. Pepper."

The engine of the backhoe ground to a stop causing all three people to turn around curiously. The driver, Bob, was climbing down from his seat.

"Hey, Marnie, come over here!" he yelled.

Marnie walked in his direction with Sonya and Mr. Pepper following her. Bob turned around again and yelled, "You've got something down here!"

For a minute, the news didn't register. "Something?" Marnie blinked a few times with a quizzical look on her face.

"I think it's a body," Bob said as they crossed the paved park road and came to a standstill next to the pit. Looking down into the excavation, all four people studied the bones unearthed by the backhoe's bucket.

"That's a skull," Marnie said, kneeling down to see better.

"And that's a rib cage and a leg bone of some sort," Bob added.

No one spoke, but Sonya realized that all three dogs were sitting almost directly across from them. Willard wagged his tail weakly. She knew in an instant what that particular wag meant. He felt guilty. That was what the barking and ripping around the pit was all about. He'd seen the ghost and couldn't resist a chase.

"I'm beginning to think this park is cursed," Marnie said shaking her head. "Ghosts running about making passes at guests, and now I've probably got some type of Indian burial ground situation going on where my pool is supposed to go. I'm calling the sheriff. They'd better see this for themselves."

Chapter 6

Sonya tried to quiet her inner self. She needed to know if the ghost was still present, but she didn't get the chance. Lewis and Clark both jumped back from their sitting position to being on all fours and intensely focused on something directly in front of them.

Willard's body wiggled and his eyes flitted back and forth from Sonya's to something visible only to the dogs. Marnie's boys growled in a low, menacing way. Lewis barked. There, hovering in the middle of the pit, a rippling mirage effect was pulsating in the atmosphere. Ten to one, thought Sophie to herself, it was the interloper from last night's domestic drama.

With a furtive glance to see if anyone else saw the female shape taking form, Sonya realized the rest of the party were oblivious to the apparition. She sent out another push like she'd done earlier when she was in the camper. This time, the spirit locked on to her instantly.

"My name is Sonya. Who are you?" Sonya said without speaking.

The ghost lifted its head as if it was going to howl at the sky. It let out a wail. All three dogs barked excitedly and looked for ways to scramble down the side of the pit's slope.

"No! Lewis and Clark!" Marnie commanded. "Come here!"

Feeling a wave of pity for the poor thing, now beginning to evaporate, Sonya tried to slow its disappearance. "I'm sorry. Maybe I can help you if you'll let me," she said mentally.

For a slight moment, it paused and appeared to think about the offer. It shook its head and disappeared. Sonya thought of Fritz. If he were here, he might be able to help. The eternal question regarding Fritz was; where was he? Fritz had a terrible habit of popping off when you needed him most. She looked for an inconspicuous place to slip off to where she might try to call Fritz. Spotting a washroom and toilet facility, she excused herself. Marnie was busy talking with Bob and Dale, the park's handyman, who'd walked over to see what the commotion was about.

Willard fell in step beside her, occasionally glancing up at her face. Once they were out of earshot, Sonya said, "Willy, I can't fault a terrier for enjoying a good chase, but you've got to learn that ghosts aren't afraid of you, sweetie. You could have been hurt if you'd fallen into that huge hole. Better to come find me next time, okay?"

Willy's guilty trot returned to its usual buoyancy. He showed his eager affection by asking to be picked up with a two paw high-ten at the back of Sonya's leg. She picked him up and went inside the toilet/washroom facility. Fortunately, no one was around, so with Willard in her arms, Sonya called, "Fritz! Where are you? I need your help, right now!" No response came from the universe.

"Fritz, I know you can hear me. I think I've found the ghost we're looking for."

Fritz materialized looking aghast at the surroundings. "*You* are looking for, my dear. I'm happy to interact only on a modest scale with my own kind. What is this sad place you're living in, my love?"

Sonya sighed. Her lovable Scottish specter's memory wasn't always the best. "I don't live here, Fritz," Sonya said exasperatedly. She decided on a different approach. "Where have you been?"

"That ridiculous great-great-great grandson of mine who currently calls himself the nineteenth Lord Dunbar is turning my home into a wallowing hole for the addle-brained tourist hordes. That's where I've been."

Fritz stomped around the tight laundry room and tried to kick an unsuspecting cart. Instead of sending the laundry cart flying, his ghost foot went through the spokes of the wheel frustrating him even more, so he continued his temper tantrum.

"He's a nincompoop of the worst order. My family crypt is being turned into a wine cellar and the gardens are playing host to longhaired, emaciated troubadours who scream and strum ridiculous ballads about their anxious lives. I'd be anxious, too, Sunny, if I forgot how to bathe and where to get a good shave."

"You don't bathe, Fritz. You're a ghost. What do you mean about the troubadours?" Sunny asked.

"They're these sad looking fellows telling miserable love stories with instruments much like a guitar while hundreds of gyrating followers watch them scream, writhe, and hop about a stage. It's most disconcerting and somewhat shocking."

"I think you must have witnessed a rock concert, Fritz. Your grandson is probably finding new ways to create revenue. It may be your home, but it's his responsibility now."

Fritz slumped onto a toilet seat. "It's hard to let go of your home, Sunny, even for a ghost."

Sonya patted him on the shoulder. "That's why you need to be occupied. Help me find The Whispering Pines' ghost and it will take your mind off things back home."

Fritz smiled and gazed up at Sonya with a smitten look. "I do love you, lass. Your ghost is my ghost. Where was it last?"

"I last saw her floating above a massive hole in the earth right outside this toilet. What say we toddle out and take a look together? There are a few people milling about, so please don't pull any funny business, okay?"

Standing at full attention, Fritz saluted, saying, "It's a privilege to serve."

With Willard leading the way, they all three exited the toilet/laundry and stepped back over to the pit. The sound of car tires crunching on the gravel made everyone look up to see who was arriving. It was Sheriff Zeb Walker with one of his deputies, Tommy Kirchner. Neither looked exactly thrilled as they got out of the police vehicle. Sonya quickly checked to see if Fritz was still with her, which he was, but doing odd calisthenics, which she supposed were being done to bring him into contact with the ghost. She rolled her eyes and turned around as the sheriff addressed Marnie.

"Well, Marnie, when did you start tossing the unpaid guests into your pit?"

"Zeb, give me some credit. I'd do better than my backyard if I wanted to get rid of someone," Marnie retorted.

The tall, easy-going police official adjusted his hat and said, "And that's why I won't be dragging you down to the office today. I've always thought of you as the responsible type when it came to illicit body disposal."

"Quit trying to charm me today, Zeb. I'm not in the mood."

Willow Valley's Sheriff stood about six foot three inches with jet-black hair beginning to turn white at the temples. There was nothing weakly or wanting in his physique. He was about forty-five years old and when he wasn't wrestling criminals, he was busting broncs on the local rodeo circuit or hauling hay to his hundred head of cattle. His uniform, if you could call it one, was a relaxed rendition of the more official looking ones his officers were expected to wear.

"The County's sending a forensic team down from Pineville. Bob, you did the right thing. If you would, back your backhoe up so that Tommy and I can tape off the site. Marnie, you'll need to keep guests from blocking the area for probably the next three days. I can't be sure when the boys in Pineville will get here, but it won't be too long."

Marnie shook her head and thanked Zeb. Turning to Sonya, she asked, "Will you keep me posted, if you find... anyone?"

"Find anyone?" Zeb asked, a hint of amusement in his voice. "Have you lost somebody else, Marnie?"

Marnie's expression showed she wasn't sure about openly admitting to hiring a ghost hunter or discussing last night's high-spirited commotion, but she plunged in anyway.

"Zeb, this is Mrs. Sonya Caruthers, our community's ghost whisperer. The Pines had a...well, for lack of a better word, a phenomenon, happen last night and I've asked her to look into it."

The Sheriff smiled and offered his hand to Sonya. When their hands touched, Sonya felt a tiny zap of electricity.

"I've been a fan of that TV series about ghost hunters since it first came out. I'll be honest with you Mrs. Caruthers, I'm not much of a believer in that kind of stuff, but it sure is fun to get the shivers once in a while."

Sonya smiled at the Sheriff. "There're ghosts everywhere, and some are with us as watchful, protecting spirits. They aren't always visible and some are barely perceptible. They leave a faint trace of energy, but even I get the shivers sometimes, too, Sheriff."

"I'll leave the ghosts to you, Mrs. Caruthers. I've got enough problems dealing with the living," Zeb said with a charming smile. He turned to Marnie, saying, "We will get that tape up. Let's keep the dogs and curious types out of the pit, if you can."

"I'll do my best, Zeb," Marnie said with a sigh, "but we have quite a number of pet residents."

"Don't worry, Marnie," Dale, her handyman, said. "I'll keep guard. No ghosties or four-legged critters will get past me."

Fritz blew up behind Dale and puffed air at the back of his gray head, causing Dale to turn around and give the three dogs watching the scene an accusing look.

Willard, Lewis, and Clark were again sitting by the pit watching Fritz do weird gyrations, but with Dale's grimacing stare at them, they all three laid down with their muzzles resting on their front paws.

"Is that another one of those things?" Clark asked Lewis in regard to Fritz.

"Looks like it, but this one acts...weird," Lewis agreed.

"That's the one that lives at my house," Willard said tragically. "He's a trickster. Keep an eye on him, boys, cause he'll try and get you in trouble."

Lewis and Clark narrowed their eyes at Fritz and watched him sit down in the police car.

"Ladies, if you'll excuse me," Zeb said, "we need to get to work and you..." he addressed Marnie with a touch of teasing in his voice, "must need to get back to your ghost hunting."

As he uttered his last two words, all the electronic devices on the police vehicle blasted to life at once. Sirens screamed, lights flashed, and the radio rocked a song from an old movie, "If there's something strange in your neighborhood, who you gonna call?"

Chapter 7

The group stared dumbfounded at the blaring light show.
Zeb and Tommy hustled over to the car and, finding no one
inside, immediately started turning off switches.

"Did you see someone in this car?" Zeb shouted in a
flustered manner back to Marnie, Mr. Pepper, and Sonya.
"You've got a prankster running about. There's no way all
of these can turn on at the same time."

Marnie and Sonya looked at Mr. Pepper. "We've got a
prankster all right," Sonya said, "but it's probably not the
same one from last night's camper hoopla."

Sonya walked off toward the police car. She would
need to reel Fritz in without speaking out loud. Fritz sat
laughing and enjoying himself in the front seat of the
vehicle. Every time Zeb or Tommy turned off a switch,
another one would be flipped on sending the horn or the
lights back into life.

Sonya looked around to see where Willard was, but all
three dogs were gone. The noise from the sirens probably
sent them scooting under the nearest camper. She pursed
her lips firmly and told Fritz mentally to stop the antics.
The car became completely silent. A brisk wind blew
around the car sending both officers' hats flying, forcing

the men to give chase.

"Fritz, did you have any luck with the ghost?"

"No, she's a silly bit, Sunny. Ran off in that direction." He pointed towards a wooded area.

"Thank you for trying. I'll see you back at the house. Be good and run along," Sonya said firmly in her head. She heard Fritz's whisper right next to her ear. It startled her slightly making both Mr. Pepper and Marnie give her a perplexed look.

"I just wanted them to know you weren't a charlatan, Sunny. The cowboy's tone was sarcastic. He's not so sure any longer, is he? You should do some mumbo-jumbo stuff while I turn all the light on again until they beg you to make it stop."

"You're going to get me arrested, Fritz. Be good and if you don't want to go home, help look for the ghost."

"She's not here," he said in a bored tone, "I told you she went over to the trees. Maybe she's a Trow. They like to groan and moan a lot. In Scotland, they, too, were undead spirits who were always looking for a spot at the hearth to warm themselves." Feeling a light kiss on her cheek, she knew Fritz was gone.

"I don't know what the heck got into this car," Sheriff Walker said while sitting in the car. Looking up at Sonya, he said, "Mrs. Caruthers, you don't have a sidekick pulling strings somewhere do you?"

Sonya laughed, "You'd be surprised, Sheriff, you really would. I'm sure whoever or whatever is having fun with you is gone."

The Sheriff shook his head back and forth. "Well, the last few days down this road have kept the Department hopping; that's for sure. The old Turner house burned down two nights ago."

"I bet it was someone looking for the old Turner treasure, Sheriff," Dale said while resting his weight up against the police vehicle. "Do you remember the Turner girls? They were real lookers in their day. Whatever happened to them?"

Zeb kept his attention on the dashboard of his car. "I was a deputy at the time, Dale. Some people think one daughter took her mama's money and ran off with a man from Springville. The other one got off to somewhere like Australia, but I didn't pay much attention. Guess that's why they never came back, too many people would have been prone to gossip."

Dale's expression didn't hint at any worry over gossiping town folks.

"Still, everyone thought the one named Poppy ran off with Ryan Houseman. She, Poppy that is, was the reason he broke off his relationship with Kathy Berkowitz." Dale shook his head at the tragedy of the situation. "There've been plenty of people who thought the Turner house might hold more than a few secrets, if not a stash of money."

The police vehicle's siren whirred to again making Dale's backend spring forward from its resting spot on the fender. This time, everyone laughed and Zeb said, "I'm beginning to believe in Marnie's ghost. One thing is for sure, this ghost has perfect timing."

"I'll leave this pit and its body in your capable hands,

Zeb," Marnie said with a sigh. "I've got plenty to keep me busy. The Whispering Pines is hosting a barbecue competition in the next few weeks and I want the place shipshape."

"Do you mind if I follow you, Marnie? I've got a few things I need to ask," Sonya asked.

"You bet. Let's have a nice cup of coffee. I need one and I just made donuts."

The three dogs in their hiding spot under a neighboring camper sprang to life at the word 'donuts'. They wagged their tails and did a few front paw weight shifts showing their enthusiasm for Marnie's suggestion.

"Come on, Willard. Follow us," Lewis said, his happiness lighting up his soft brown eyes.

"Oh, yeah," Clark joined in with his tail high and wagging joyfully, "Mom makes great donuts and she shares with us. They're sweet and taste like a big, fluffy cookie."

Willard loved sweet treats. He didn't get them often. Usually, they were given after he'd been to the vet. A donut was something extremely special. He eagerly watched Sonya and Marnie walk toward the tour bus-sized RV that the two beagles called home. Falling in step happily with the boys, he trotted off to a donut he hoped he wouldn't have to share with anyone.

Chapter 8

Though it was May, as anyone from southern Missouri can tell you, it is usually already hot enough for people to need their air conditioners on. As the menagerie of two humans and three dogs scrambled into Marnie's roomy RV, a nice waft of cool air welcomed them.

"Make yourself at home," Marnie said and pointed at the cozy dining banquette "Have a seat. I'm going to brew some coffee."

Sonya had an immediate sense of easy-going relaxed homeyness in Marnie's four-wheel house. There were pictures of Lewis and Clark as adorable puppies and one with them sitting with Santa on a big sleigh. Books were neatly piled in stacks and tucked into easy-to-reach places so if one was ever in need of a literary fix, something to read was always close at hand. The boys' doggy toys had their place in a basket under the built in desk and a delicious lingering scent of many happy meals prepared and shared permeated the space, making Sonya excited to try one of Marnie's homemade donuts.

The three dogs made themselves comfortable, as well. Lewis and Clark jumped up into two upholstered, swivel chairs opposite the banquette. Willard sat by Sonya's feet under the table. He knew not to jump on other people's furniture unless he'd been given the go-ahead by Sonya.

"I made these yesterday. It's my mother's recipe. There are donut holes, too. Some donuts have powdered sugar and some are without. Which is your favorite?" Marnie asked.

She put two pretty plates down in front of Sonya. Both supported a perfect pyramid of deep fried delights. All three dogs' tails wagged furiously.

"I love both. They are so pretty with a sprinkling of sugar, though," Sonya said smiling happily. Like most people who are presented with something that promises to be tasty and memorable, she couldn't help but be delighted by the prospect of trying both kinds.

Marnie put two cups of coffee down on the table, each with a spoon nestled in its saucer. She offered Sonya a bright yellow cotton napkin and asked, "Do you care for cream or sugar in your coffee?"

"Both, thank you."

Once both women were sitting, Marnie asked, "Sonya, would Willard like a donut hole?"

Sonya smiled, while at the same time noting the hopeful expressions on each dog's face. "It would be a cold heart indeed who ignored those sweet faces," she said. Selecting one with powdered sugar, she handed it to Willard, while, at the same time, both Lewis and Clark received theirs from Marnie. The boys, in typical dog fashion, swallowed the round treat in one gulp and smiled, open-mouthed as if in hopes of another. It was always difficult not to give in to dog cuteness and hand a second treat over, especially when they had white grins from the sugar.

"That's enough, boys," Marnie said simply. "Go find your beds." Both dogs hopped down from the swivel chairs and dutifully curled up in their beds. Willard watched them and settled himself on the floor next to Sonya's feet.

As the two women sipped the hazelnut coffee and enjoyed the homemade donuts, they each learned something about the other's life. Marnie told Sonya how she was new to running an RV park but not to barbecue competitions. She explained about her idea of having a pool at the park. It would be an excellent amenity for her guests, and the best location was next to the grand pavilion.

"Who would have thought someone would bury a body here," she said, stirring her second cup of coffee.

"It's sad to think of some poor person dumped that way. No wonder you have a ghost problem. I'm surprised you didn't have issues before now," Sonya said.

"That's true. Why didn't I? It's been so quiet here, that is, until this morning, and it wasn't until today that Bob got busy digging the hole for the pool. If it was the ghost of the body we found today, shouldn't it have come to life before?"

"Typically, a spirit will stay close to either the place where they died or, in most cases, their home." Sonya thought back to her conversation with Fritz earlier in the laundry. He was attached to his home and had been upset over the changes taking place there.

"Why don't we do a ghost intervention tonight?" Sonya said with excitement in her voice.

"I thought that was what we were doing now," Marnie replied with her coffee cup poised halfway between the table and her mouth.

"Yes, but I'd like to do something more along the line of a few people coming together to bring the ghost to us."

"A séance?"

"If you want to call it that, yes."

"Well, why not? Sounds kind of fun. Who should we invite and where do you want to have it?"

"Here would be good. The pavilion is perfect. It's nice this time of year." Sonya looked at the three dogs resting with their eyes shut. "Would it be okay to leave the dogs in your camper?"

"Sure, I'll see if Mr. Pepper is up for coming and I'll bring Dale and another friend who lives here named Julia. That gives us four. Do you think that's enough?" Marnie asked.

"Five would be better and perhaps another man."

"I'll ask Noah Simpson. He's a fussy type, but he has a thing for Julia, so he'll follow her anywhere. What time?"

"Eight o'clock will work perfectly, not too late and not too early. But it should be getting dark; it's more fun that way." Sonya got up from her seat and put her coffee cup and plate in the sink. "Till then, and thank you for those incredible donuts. You and your mother have a real talent."

Sonya and Willard waved goodbye to Marnie and the rest of the men working the crime scene. The county forensic team had arrived and were busy working down in the pit. As she put on her helmet and made sure Willard was suited up safely in his crate on the back of the moped, Sonya's mind played over her conversations with Fritz and Marnie. Ghosts have attachments, too. Not generally, over their bodies but with places or people they've known and loved.

What was the story with this ghost? Was it lonely? Was the body in the pit the ghost's or someone it loved? Sonya turned the key of the moped's engine and it hummed nicely to life. She pulled the two-wheeled vehicle out onto the shady highway that led back to town. One thing was for sure, they would get some answers tonight.

Chapter 9

It was quiet and peaceful among the shady grove of trees that lined the one-lane, gravel road leading to where the house once stood. At the end, the burnt-out remains of a dwelling stood, charred and sad looking, nestled between three beautiful, ancient oaks. A number of climbing rose bushes planted before the age of poodle skirts and sock hops still clung to a slumping back fence barely maintaining an upright position.

The entire property exhibited the typical signs of long neglect. There were tall, overgrown, weedy bushes growing along the remaining foundations of the house. Creeping vines clung to the limestone fireplace that rose from the fallen structural remains of the once grand home of the Turner family.

The last of the day's cheerful sunlight dappled across the wild, lush springtime vegetation. A few bird families chirped and busied themselves with building their nests high in the trees or within the rafters of the old barn that still stood to the rear of the property.

In fact, life and all its perplexities, joys, and labors had altered little with the burning of the house. The animals, insects, and plant life were managing, as they'd always done, perfectly fine. There'd been only one displaced individual since the fire, and that was the spirit who lost everything when the house went up in flames.

Most country people know that if a house burns down, it's important to leave the fireplace intact. The old folks believe the family ghosts need a place to rest and abide. If you tear down the bricks or stone, you leave the spirits without a home.

A pair of crows called and fussed from the top of the oak trees. Loquacious fellows, they liked to be the first to announce any unusual activity happening about a place. Something was disconcerting to them and they wanted to make sure all the rest of the inhabitants of Turner farm were well aware of the situation.

Though the wind was varied and gentle, an eddy of air whirled randomly among the ashes accompanied, occasionally, by a whispering moan. The crows, unable to stand the anomaly no longer, lifted their wings, flapping them and calling loudly to all who had ears to listen. Something wasn't right, and they, as a group, would not quietly stand by while weeping ghosts wandered. In less time than it takes to spell your name, they took flight and disappeared over the treetops in a southwesterly direction.

The last light of the day took its cue from their hurried departure so it, too, drew a last breath and faded, leaving the Turner home deadly quiet. The fretful spirit took shelter within the cold, partially soot-covered fireplace, but the loneliness of the place increased its torment causing it to quit the meager dwelling and search instead for light, warmth and human comfort.

Down the tree-lined gravel road, it went, being pulled

like a weary moth to a living flame. Not far, as the ghost remembered, was a place offering relief for all that ailed its tormented soul: The Whispering Pines RV Park, truly an oasis of calm for a sad, homeless spirit in need of a warm body to snuggle. When you're dead, you'll try anything to keep the chill of death from becoming too real and unbearable.

Chapter 10

The month of May is truly one of the most beautiful in Missouri. Temperatures are warm, but not hideously muggy like in June, July, and August. The insect population is still young, small of girth, and not yet interested in humans like they will be by August and September.

Flowers can be found still blooming on crabapple trees, plum trees, and dogwood trees, while as soon as the last frost can be verified, people joyfully begin filling window boxes, outdoor pots, and yards with flowering plants of every imaginable kind.

Along Sonya's street called Pickwick, the quest for the best yard had reached its zenith. Residents, already blessed with one-hundred-year-old trees and car-sized snowball hydrangea bushes, had added their own touches, such as climbing roses or wisteria artfully pruned over trellises or clinging effortlessly along front porches.

The lovely original brick-paved street, like most in the historic district of Willow Valley, was lined with tall elms and oaks creating a wonderful canopy for the turn of the century houses. There was a harmony between the living and non-living elements, which made them coexist peacefully together.

Over time, the maturity of the trees and the virtue of the handsome homes had established Pickwick Place as one of Willow Valley's most beautiful and, therefore, most sought-after neighborhoods.

As proof of their American pride, proud Pickwick residents during the 1976 Bicentennial had decided to plant flowering trees known for their color such as redbud and dogwood along the street's sidewalks. With the occasional crape myrtle flaunting hues of pink, purple, white, and red, the neighborhood was blessed with even more color and charm throughout the summer months.

It was in this leafy haven that Sonya and Willard were having a simple breakfast of link sausages, sourdough toast with plum jelly and hard-boiled eggs on the front porch. The twosome sat peacefully at the outdoor dining table watching people come and go along the street.

The regularity of the mailman, the occasional dog accompanied by its human and the arrival of a service person or two, allowed the two sleepy breakfasters to peacefully watch the goings on while either munching on toast or, in Sonya's case, sipping strong coffee.

"What do you suppose Mrs. Townsend is having done this week, Willard?" Sonya said half-interestedly. "That's another van from the carpet and tile store. I bet she's finishing up her bathroom renovation."

"The old harridan, she'd be better off renovating her personality."

The coffee in Sonya's cup undulated from the slight shock of Fritz's arrival.

"Ah, Fritz, have you decided to pop back over to America?" Sonya asked teasingly.

Fritz had never come home after he left The Whispering Pines RV Park yesterday afternoon. He usually made a big to do at night if he was staying at Sonya's by chasing Willard around the downstairs and finally blowing up the stairwell singing a bawdy song about sailors. But it had been a quiet night, which meant he'd found more entertaining venues. He was quiet and didn't respond to her question, so she tried a second time.

"So," Sonya said, while looking the word 'harridan' up on her tablet, "why are you so grumpy this morning?" She found the definition, which meant Fritz considered Mrs. Townsend a foul-tempered, disreputable old woman. Sonya waited for his reply. He continued to brood about something.

"Fritz? You typically make caustic comments about my neighbors when you've either played poorly in Monte Carlo or heard more disconcerting news regarding your family."

"It was neither, my dear. I've been playing bridge with some old friends in Edinburgh. My friend, Dr. Samuel Winfield, though at one time a brilliant surgeon, is a complete ninny at bidding his hand."

"Were you his partner?"

"Yes, that is, until we were all relieved from continued play due to a sudden realization by Dudley Aikens, an old school chum and an excellent darts player, that his wife was about to storm the house in a jealous rage over Dudley's philandering with a Tahitian maid."

"My, how you ghosts do get around once you're dead," Sonya exclaimed. "How did old Dudley meet a Tahitian girl in Edinburgh?"

"Not in Edinburgh, dear Sunny, he met her at a Tahitian farewell ceremony. With flowers and beautiful songs to say goodbye, it was, I suppose, romantic," Fritz said sitting down on the railing of the porch.

"Romantic? That's a new way of looking at a funeral. What was he doing there?"

"He was doing a bit of afterlife travel and witnessed the ceremony and decided to observe from a discrete distance. He'd been an avid socialist during his heyday, but with death, he was becoming more of a humanist. He likes to study different cultures and write lengthy tomes on the value of human life." Fritz gave a martyred sigh and continued. "Dudley said he suddenly saw this exquisitely beautiful woman step out of her tree trunk coffin, and poor Dudley was smitten. He introduced himself and they've been together ever since."

"That's a lot to take in, Fritz. I thought the afterlife would be more…well, spiritual," Sonya said with a hint of humor in her voice.

"Oh, it can be, of course, dear, but some people choose a different path. Diversity is good," Fritz said, smiling like the Cheshire cat.

"Why, look Fritz, it's a police car driving down the street. It's slowing down."

"And it appears the young constable is visiting the Gorgon next door."

"Fritz! You're terrible sometimes. Give Mrs. Townsend a break."

Sonya watched the policeman stop the car and step out onto the pavement. "He's coming up the sidewalk, Fritz, and we say police officer, not constable. I'll wave. I'd love to know if they've found any more information on the dead person."

"Po-tay-to, po-tah-to, to-may-to, to-mah-to, who cares what they're called. I'm off. Ta-ta, for now." Fritz left, but not before brushing Sonya's cheek with a light kiss.

Tommy Kirchner, Willow Valley's Deputy Sheriff, was a tall, lean, young man in his late twenties. Born and raised in the same town he now served, Tommy knew everyone and their situation. He'd come to pay an official visit to Mrs. Townsend, Sonya's neighbor, who claimed she was being toyed with by aliens.

"Deputy!" Sonya called waving to him. He turned around, smiled broadly, and returned her friendly greeting.

"Hello, Mrs. Caruthers. How are you today?" he called back to her, stopping before he crossed the road.

"Do you have a minute, Deputy? I have some coffee and a freshly made cherry cheese danish if you'd care to join me."

Tommy's progress across the street was firmly arrested by the mention of homemade bakery items. A crummy cup of instant coffee had been his breakfast that morning, and that was consumed as he drove to work. Hunger won out. Visiting with Mrs. Townsend about aliens hovering outside her windows, harassing her with noises and puffs of air on the back of her head, could wait a few more minutes.

"I'd love a cup. It's been an early morning of duties already and your offer is greatly appreciated," he said climbing the front steps of Sonya's tidy house. "You have a beautiful home, Mrs. Caruthers. I remember, as a boy, there being a sheepdog who lived here. He always came to the gate for a visit when I walked this way to school."

Sonya poured the Deputy a steaming cup of coffee and put a particularly well-proportioned slice of danish on a delicate fine bone china plate and handed it to him. His eyes lit up and for a moment Sonya felt a guilty for plying him with sweet treats for information, but she reminded herself he did need something to carry him through the morning.

"Yes, I have found many discarded dog toys buried in this yard. This house must have been home to many generations of humans and their pets. Do you have a special pet, Deputy?" Sonya asked while helping the young man with the cream and sugar for his coffee.

"No, unfortunately, however, our station is supposed to be getting a canine unit which will mean a German Shepherd and all the training that goes along with it. I've told Zeb, I want to take on that role."

"How nice!" Sonya cooed. "Working in such a high-demand and dangerous field can be lonely sometimes, but I feel…" Sonya studied the young man's face as he held his coffee cup halfway to his mouth, "that two special souls will be coming into your life soon."

Tommy put his cup down on the table after he took a sip. He gave Sonya a shy smile and said, "I wouldn't turn that down, ma'am. Believe it or not, it's hard to have much of a relationship in this line of work. That's why I haven't adopted a dog, too busy."

"Not to worry, Deputy. I see two gentle souls in your future. Both have been mistreated, so you'll need to be true."

For a short few minutes, they both quietly enjoyed the fresh morning atmosphere of pretty Pickwick slowly coming to life. Cars made their way down the brick road and children walked with either an older sibling or a parent down the sidewalks on their way to school. Off in the distance, a siren wailed, probably going to the hospital on the other side of town.

Tommy, full of danish and feeling relaxed, offered a morsel of gratuitous information. "The body is a woman's. Early-thirties. Cranium has a nasty dent, but they think what killed her was a fall. Her spine is broken. She's been there a while, probably around a year. Of course, you didn't hear that from me."

Sonya maternally patted Tommy's shoulder. "The ghost that has been giving The Whispering Pines its excitement lately is a female. She became active before the pool digging operation, and if your forensics are correct, as I'm sure they are, something else caused her to wake up."

Tommy laughed while shaking his head. "I kind of like the idea of working with a psychic, Mrs. Caruthers. Any idea who she is?"

"No, but I might be a bit closer after tonight."

"Oh, yeah? How do you figure that?" Tommy asked.

"We're having a group spiritual therapy session this evening at The Whispering Pines."

"Is that a fancy way of saying séance?"

Another failed approach at finding a more politically correct way to say séance. She let out a resigned sigh and said, "Yes, a séance, Tommy. Want to come? You could be that much wiser about the possible identity of the person who has been calling the pit their final resting spot this last year."

"We have our own theory, ma'am."

"More danish?"

He smiled at her bribe. "Not necessary, Mrs. Caruthers. Not many women have gone missing who also meet the age parameters of the one found in the pit."

"Would it be the woman Marnie's handyman mentioned? What was her name? Poppy, I think."

"That's one of them," Tommy agreed, "but we won't know for sure until we check the teeth against the dental records. There's one problem, though, with the Poppy Turner suggestion."

"What?"

"She's not exactly a missing person."

Chapter 11

Tommy stood up from the white wicker table and adjusted his police cap back on his head. "You see, Poppy Turner was married to a fellow named Richard Mitchell, who, by the way, still lives here in Willow Valley. He claims Poppy ran off with a guy from Springville, Missouri. Supposedly, he has a signed divorce document dated from about six months after Poppy left Willow Valley."

"So, even if it's not Poppy, any other possible leads?" Sonya asked.

"Like I said, we're working with the two dentists in town who were practicing at the time. We should know something in a few days." Tommy stepped down a few of the front porch steps. "Thank you, Mrs. Caruthers, for a delicious breakfast. I'll be seeing you. Best of luck on your séance tonight. If you learn anything," Tommy smiled impishly, "you'll return the favor?"

"Absolutely."

Tommy finished ambling down the front steps and waved at Sonya from the gate. He waited for the traffic to pass and hustled across the street and up another well-groomed front walk. Mrs. Townsend opened the door and let him in, while Sonya briskly collected her breakfast dishes onto a tray and walked inside to do the washing up.

"Are you coming, Willard or are you staying outside? The boy will be by in a few minutes who rides the skateboard. That always sends you into a frenzy."

Willard's ears perked up and he cocked his head from one side to the other as if trying to understand Sonya's meaning.

"Go ahead, but stay away from the fence. I'm not sure I trust him. He delights in getting you worked up each morning and I'm pretty sure he's the one who egged you."

The coolness of the inside rooms gave Sonya a happy pleasure. She preferred cool days to the extreme heat. Every summer halfway through the month of June, Sonya turned her keys over to a gentle mouse of a woman named Bette. From June through September, Bette managed the garden and lived in Sonya's house, taking care of things while Sonya went to Cornwall, England to get out of the heat.

After putting the kitchen to rights, she finished the rest of her housekeeping duties and went upstairs to get ready. Her hair was always a simple affair. It was short enough that a good brushing, some mousse to scrunch up the curls and maybe a clip to hold it out of her eyes produced the carefree style she admired. A bright pink tunic paired with yellow pedal pushers and pink canvas tennis shoes completed her ensemble. She put on pearl earrings, her signature piece of jewelry, and dabbed some perfume on each of her wrists and behind each ear.

"Willard!" she called from her bedroom window, "It's time to run some errands. Meet me in the kitchen!"

True to his loyal nature, Willard was waiting dutifully near the pantry door. Sonya produced the treat he always received when he followed commands, and they headed out to the moped. Ten minutes later, they were scooting along Pickwick and turning down Main Street toward Puggly's grocery store.

Scene Break

The morning was always a wonderful time for the two beagles, Lewis and Clark. Fresh smells, cool brisk air, and the anticipation of bacon or sausage for breakfast nurtured their already happy dispositions. Fortunately, for the boys, one of their absolute favorite meats was on the menu: pork. They'd each been given a whole piece of bacon by doting mom, Marnie, and afterwards, it was time to check out the park, patrol the area for marauding squirrels, and, of course, remark their territory for the one-hundredth time.

As they rounded the back of their own camper, their noses picked up a smell that both intrigued them and caused them a slight bit of anxiety. Being fairly new to the world, there were a few scents they hadn't yet learned. This one was extremely strong, causing the dogs to go into a frenzy of sniffing to find the trail.

"Whatever this is, Clark," Lewis said, "even a cat could smell it."

"Yeah, even a cat, Lewis," Clark agreed following his brother around a trashcan and down a manicured gravel path to where the open pit sat. There in the bottom of the

pit, sniffing around, was an extremely grumpy skunk. It had probably been working the campsite all night and perhaps had gotten too close to the pit's edge and had fallen in. Though it had tried to claw its way up one side and then another, the loose dirt and rock always repeatedly made it lose its grip and tumble back down.

The boys watched the animal in wonder, and with every fiber in their bodies, they wished to scramble down and give the interloper what for. But every time they neared the edge, their footing would give way and force them to scoot back to save themselves from plunging downward. The next best thing to do in this situation was bark and the louder, the better.

Most of the residents of The Whispering Pines RV Park were early risers and had already been up, taken their walk and had their breakfast, but for one. Mr. Noah Simpson was still snuggled up in his warm bed that morning because the night before he'd been out dancing with another resident, Julia Abercrombie. The pair had been out until midnight. Lewis and Clark's barking, so close to his own camper, was having a decided effect on his ability to stay in a deep sleep.

Finally, Mr. Simpson rolled over and stuffed a pillow over his head in an effort to drown out the yapping. It was at that moment, he realized he wasn't alone. His mind experienced a sort of jolt. Had the lovely Julia whom he'd been trying to woo for over six months come home with him last night? He forced his sleeping brain to focus. He couldn't remember. His grogginess kept him from being able to access the exact details of their parting after the dance.

Feeling the weight of a body curled up next to him, he congratulated himself on his masculine prowess. Though he tried desperately, to no avail, to recall the exciting specifics, he decided it was safe to go ahead and murmur, "Darling, good morning."

The responding cooing sound, typical of a sleepy woman waking up, confirmed for him it must, indeed, be Julia. With his joy running over, he reached for the bundled form that was well covered by his heavy comforter. Pulling back the bed cover, Noah bent down to whisper something enticing in his bedmate's ear and steal a morning kiss from her warm neck. To his utter astonishment and heart-wrenching horror, he realized nothing was there. A pair of cold, clammy, yet invisible, hands applied themselves to his face holding his head still while a pair of unearthly lips pressed against his own. Poor Noah screamed at the top of his manly lungs and bolted from his bed and his camper until he found himself panting hysterically at the far edge of his own camping lot.

The scream attracted the attention of Lewis and Clark, as well as Marnie and Mr. Pepper, who were both outside. They came scurrying over to where Noah rested, leaning against one of the massive pine trees shading his lot. He tried to compose himself, but upon looking down, realized he was wearing only his boxers and a t-shirt advertising one of the state's baseball teams.

"What happened, Mr. Simpson?" Marnie asked, keeping her eyes courteously above waist level.

"I...I...I don't know," Noah stumbled vocally. "I think

there was someone in there but…"

Marnie and Mr. Pepper exchanged rapid, but furtive glances. Neither one moved, but Mr. Pepper sighed deeply.

"I'm afraid, old friend, you may have had a visitor of a ghostly nature. What you need is a cup of coffee, and," he glanced at Noah's lack of trousers, "something to take the chill off."

Noah, who by any standard of men's couture, was always at the top of his game when it came to his clothes, hair, and presentation, saw himself in total dishabille and, for a second time that morning, his system was in shock.

"Oh, my God! I'm practically asking to be charged with indecent exposure." He headed for his camper's door but came to a full stop. His hesitation was relieved by Marnie's quick perception of his situation.

"Mr. Simpson, why don't you go with Mr. Pepper to his camper? I'm sure he has something you can wear and maybe something to eat." The look she shot Pepper indicated he didn't have a choice in the matter, and soon, both men were heading across the park's central gravel road toward breakfast and warm pants.

"I'm glad we're getting this sorted out tonight," she said under her breath giving the camper a weary eye. "The sooner this spicy spook is sent on to her spiritual reward, the better."

Lewis and Clark watched Marnie stomp off in the direction of her office. In the hubbub with Noah, the skunk had finally found a toehold and bustled off to freedom and the woods. The boys approached Noah's camper with noses to the ground and ears twitching.

"That thing from yesterday is back, Clark. I can feel it."

"Makes my back itchy. I think we should stay away from it," Clark suggested.

"Hold on, there brother. Something is rattling around in there."

Lewis and Clark hunkered down on the ground under Noah's camper. Above them, they heard things hitting the floor and weird singing. The ghost broke free from the camper and was heading through the park. The boys followed at a safe distance.

"Let's see where it goes," Lewis said.

Even though they knew better than to leave the park, they watched the specter head into the woods.

"We're not supposed to go in there, Lewis," Clark warned.

"I know, but if we were to follow it, we'd be helping Mom."

After a thirty minute wander through an open wooded area, the boys saw a burned down house. The ghost was nowhere in sight, but something was disturbing the crows settled on the old stone chimney.

"Look! Those birds are worried," Clark pointed out.

"That's our thing. She must live here when she's not out haunting our park. Let's get home and send out a message to Willard."

Lewis and Clark, using their excellent noses, found

their way back to The Whispering Pines RV Park. Within minutes, the canine system of sending news was put into operation. The bloodhound known as Rusty barked and howled getting the attention of the Husky, who lived down the road toward town. He, in turn, informed the two crazy, car-chasing bull terriers who waited for Lou, the Chihuahua, to come by with the mailman. They barked the story as Lou's owner drove by with them in hot pursuit. Once Lou made it to town, he would make sure he talked with the dog in question.

Lou sent a message back through the dog-line saying he'd see Willard around two o'clock. That's when they worked his street. In less time than it takes to slap something up on a human social media site, the dogs of Willow Valley had effectively gotten the word out.

Chapter 12

Puggly's was a throwback to another time when grocery stores were not the dazzling, streamlined, consumer Shangri-Las most suburbanites have come to expect in today's shopping experience. Instead, it was like walking into a place straight out of our collective American small town memory.

Not tidy by any means, but the shelves were stocked with such a variety of things that one could gaze with childlike wonder at items thought long since removed from the American-made product vernacular. But Puggly's proved they hadn't disappeared. They'd simply been supplanted by bright techno gadgets made in countries halfway around the ever-shrinking globe.

At Puggly's, kids picked from a wonderful variety of great American-made items. They bought, or needled their adults to buy for them: Candy and toys still being turned out by people in places like Pennsylvania, New Jersey, Georgia, and Oregon. Wooden yo-yos and a game with plastic monkeys shared the shelf with a set of real wooden blocks for building and a brightly colored tin kaleidoscope that, when put to the eye and lifted to the sun, would dazzle even the most jaded video game junkie. A kazoo and one-penny bubble gum, along with taffy made not far from

Willow Valley by two ladies who brought their candy in once a week packed in the back of their old Ford Bronco. All promised simpler forms of childhood pleasures.

There wasn't a rule against well-behaved dogs coming into Puggly's. Most people in Willow Valley knew whether their dog was capable of handling the situation or not. In small places, people still uphold the dictates of good manners and common courtesy toward others and property. There were the occasional times when someone's teenager might express a rebel action or a tourist would confusedly forget they weren't in DC or LA and wonder why it took so long for something to be done, but common sense could be counted on to usually prevail and tolerance was a sign of good breeding.

Pets of an anxious nature were leashed outside to one of the many shady areas reserved for this circumstance. Willard, for all his good attributes, found going into Puggly's a place of anxious odor-overdrive. The smell of fresh meat, bakery items, and bags of dog food, cat food, and even goat food in the back of the market, caused Willard to become too excited. Sonya always left him in his basket with an umbrella opened over his crate to keep him cool. He waited patiently and solicited any greetings or gentle pats from the regular stream of pedestrians.

With Sonya inside doing her shopping, people and kids came and went. Not far from his position on the back of the moped, was tied a sleek Greyhound.

"Hi Lucky," Willard said. "How's the rheumatism?"

"I'm terribly grateful it's finally warming up. This winter, I hardly moved from my electric blanket."

"Well, you're looking fit. Where did you get the sweater?"

"A lady is making them. Glad you like it. It's been a godsend."

While the two chatted, the mailman pulled up in front of Puggly's. There in the window, perched on his padded seat was Lou, the Chihuahua.

"Morning, Willard. Lucky." Lou leaned out of the window. "I've got some news for you, Willard, from the boys down at The Whispering Pines."

"What's up, Lou?" Willard asked, fairly curious because he rarely got mail.

"Lewis and Clark say they need to talk with you soon. There's a ghost wandering about the place and they think they know where it lives. Sorry, to hear about it, Willard. Those things give me the shakes."

"Thanks, Lou. I'll be seeing them tonight. Sonya's got some sort of ghost encounter planned. I wish she'd give the one living at our house the boot."

Lou and Lucky shook their heads in thoughtful commiseration.

"Here comes the boss," Lou said, seeing the mailman, Felix Tushman, coming back out of Puggly's.

"Thanks again, Lou. Take care. By the way, have you seen that boy who rides the skateboard around today?"

"Sure have. He just left the library and was heading down Pickwick."

"Gripes! I wish Sonya would get a move on. That kid is worse than fleas."

"See ya, boys!" Lou called as the mail truck fired back up and pulled out of the grocery parking lot.

The moped shook causing Willard, his umbrella, and the crate he called Shotgun to career dangerously back and forth. Willard refused to give Fritz the pleasure of seeing him stress pant. Sonya, fortunately, breezed out of the grocery store's entrance and witnessed the shaking moped.

"Fritz! Be good and tell Willard you're sorry," Sonya commanded. "You're about to lose privileges. You think the family in Scotland can be difficult."

Fritz knew when he'd fiddled too much with the Willard situation. So, he patted the terrier on the head causing it to move up and down in a weird way. Lucky, watching the scene from his spot, barked worriedly at Fritz's unearthly energy. Sonya sighed and hopped back on her moped.

"Boys, be good for ten minutes until we get home. Fritz, are you riding with us?"

Putting himself on the handlebars, he pulled out a riding crop from his belt and waved it. "Let us make haste, woman! To home!" He pointed the crop forward and stabbed at the air as if to indicate it was time to move.

"Such a drama king, Fritz," Sonya said and tapped the horn to give him a start. The moped hummed to life and the three friends zipped down the street with Fritz as acting moped mascot.

Once back home, Sonya flung her helmet, purse, and keys down on the wooden bench in the kitchen. She told Willard and Fritz to leave her alone for a while. It was time to do some digging into Willow Valley's missing persons' past. She needed to find out more about the past than what Deputy Kirchner shared earlier at breakfast.

It took some time to dig through the library's online site and Willow Valley's local paper's online archive. The town had the usual crimes for one of its size, but no one had gone missing during the last year. The Whispering Pines' ghost must be from another situation. Good thing they'd scheduled the séance. This would be the best way to try to learn more about the unhappy soul looking for love in all the wrong places.

The phone rang, and Sonya saw it was Marnie calling.

"Hey, what's up?" Sonya said into the receiver.

"Have you looked outside?" Marnie's voice said with a hint of concern in it.

Sonya peeked out her office window. Massive cauliflower-shaped thunderclouds were beginning to roll in from the West. This time of year, the weather could get nasty. She frowned and said, "Doesn't look good for a séance at your place tonight, Marnie. Let's do it over here. I've got lots of room."

"Sonya, I don't leave the boys during thunderstorms. It's too upsetting for them. Would you mind if I bring them with me?"

"Absolutely, bring them. Willard will love it. Let's pray there isn't any thunder when the séance gets going. Might give us all the willies," Sonya said with a laugh.

"I'm getting so excited. Mr. Pepper, Julia, Dale, and Noah all are coming. We had another visit this morning from the ghost. This time, it was Noah. I'd like to get this resolved before someone has a heart attack or hurts themselves fleeing from their ghoulish experience."

"Oh, boy, she's been back? Anything new to report, such as, did she say anything? Did she materialize?"

"Sorry, but nothing new to tell you. It was the same scenario as before, except this time she snuggled up to Noah. Good thing the weather is getting warmer. He was in his undershorts when he came bolting out of his camper," Marnie said laughing.

The two women had a good giggle at the poor man's expense.

"I'm going to make a dessert that will put color back in his cheeks," Sonya said and realizing the pun, both women laughed naughtily. "You know what I meant," Sonya added after a few seconds. "We can begin at eight o'clock if that works for all of you?"

"We'll be there and thanks about me bringing Lewis and Clark. I'll see you this evening."

Marnie hung up and Sonya hopped up from her desk. She hustled downstairs to the kitchen and pulled ingredients out of her cupboard. While at Puggly's, she'd bought a few things to make a lemon cream pie, so no time like the present.

Willard meandered into the room. He had a knack for knowing when food was being prepared in the kitchen. A few whines later, he padded back out of the room with a crunchy bone to chew on as he sat in the window seat.

Sonya first made the piecrust. After years of baking, she

didn't exactly measure anymore. This much flour, a scoop of lard, a pinch of salt, and some ice-cold water went together in an ample ceramic bowl. Soon the dough was being put into the refrigerator for a short stint to firm up. After a quick trip outside to water roses, newly planted geraniums and a bed of impatiens, she went back inside and washed her hands.

Taking out the dough, she sprinkled flour on an area of her countertop and rolled out a nice round circle. Carefully laying it across a tin pie pan that had been her grandmother's, Sonya worked it into place and gave it a pretty fluting along the rim. She popped it into the oven to cook.

It was time to do the filling. Egg yolks were lightly beaten in a bowl and then cream and sugar were added. A few nice lemons were squeezed for their juice, as well. The timer on the oven went off telling her the piecrust was done. Taking it out, she sat it on a wire rack to cool. The pie filling ingredients were finished and mixed until smooth. Taking the cooled shell, she poured in the filling and gently placed the pie in the oven.

Sonya took cream, sugar, gelatin, and vanilla and whipped it in a stainless steel bowl till it made soft, fluffy peaks and put it into the fridge.

"There are a couple of things I miss about life," Fritz said close to Sonya's ear.

"Food?" Sonya asked turning around to see if Fritz was in his material form. He was standing right behind her looking down into her eyes.

"Ah, yes. I'm looking forward to the time I'm whisked

up into the heavens and my final reward is revealed to me, but man does not live by bread alone, Sunny."

"Quit getting all lovey-dovey with me, Fritz," she gave him a kiss on his cheek. "You know your dead wife doesn't like it when you flirt with other women."

"Sea hag, she was!" Fritz bellowed at the mention of his wife. "The bane of my existence, Mary MacGregor. A black heart and a blacker tongue. If she shows her brooding, wickedness in this home of blessed gentility, I will rout her with my own riding crop and shoo her like a nasty pestilence from our home."

"Are you done? You're a bit worked up over Mary today! Did you see her at the castle?" Sonya said offering Fritz a place to sit beside her at the table. She needed to keep an eye on the pie, so it was best to stay close.

"Well, since you asked, lass. Yes, Mary was about the place when I was trying to dissuade my fool of a great-great-great-grandson from turning the crypt into a place for toffs to swig wine. She ran me out of my home. Such a lot of fuss. That woman is a crazed banshee and will have it only her way."

Sonya smiled. She knew better than to get in between Fritz and his dead wife, Mary. Fritz liked to live in America because, secretly, he was a bit afraid of her. Two hundred years ago, she had ruled the roost at home and she wasn't about to give up her command so many years later. Fritz would keep trying to breach the ancestral walls of his old estate, but with Mary in residence, he wouldn't have much success.

"I think it best you try taking something nice to Mary.

Make amends and do it up right, Fritz. If you both work together, you might be able to help your great-great-grandchildren save the place financially without bringing the walls down around all of you."

Fritz considered Sonya's wise advice. He stood up and announced he'd give it a try. With the sound of the oven beeping, Fritz said his adieu and Sonya retrieved the delicious smelling pie from the oven. Willard popped his head around the corner, his round, black eyes searching for Fritz's presence. Satisfied that Sonya was alone in the kitchen, he toddled in and sat looking up at her with a beseeching gaze.

"Go play outside, Willard. The boys, Lewis and Clark, will be here later. No more treats this afternoon. I'm busy."

With a fresh, renewed vigor at the mention of Lewis and Clark's names, Willard went out to the garden and found his favorite place to watch for squirrels. With any luck, a foolish one would come along and give him a good chase. That was nature's way of keeping things tight.

Chapter 13

Sheriff Zeb Walker lounged in a reclining position in his overstuffed office chair. The morning was going well, mainly due to the delivery of two useful things: first, someone's wife had brought in a huge coffee cake for one of the officers' birthday and secondly, Pineville had already finished with some of the preliminary forensic results brought in that morning by Deputy Kirchner.

With a nice-sized portion of cinnamon and brown sugar-drizzled cake and a cup of black coffee, the Sheriff sat and munched while studying the papers in front of him. The age of the dead woman made the deeply grooved creases of the Sheriff's forehead become more pronounced. It was the first thing Kirchner mentioned that morning when he handed Zeb the file.

"Something doesn't add up, Sheriff. She's definitely a murder victim, but who?" Tommy had asked before leaving to visit with an elderly lady in the old part of town about being ogled by possible aliens through her windows. Zeb shook his head with a paternal smile on his face. People get odd ideas, he thought.

But Tommy was right, things didn't add up. The female's age was between twenty-five and thirty years. She'd been stripped of clothing, jewelry and any identifying items that might have helped the investigation. According to the forensic report, the body had been in the pit for at least a year, maybe less, making the female's remains incompletely decomposed.

What he needed was a promising match from the missing women's file. Problem was, he didn't have a match. No one had gone missing at that time from Willow Valley. He shook his head. This would mean looking at all missing persons from the region, state and probably the nation as well.

Poppy Turner Mitchell would have been a perfect candidate, but she'd never been reported missing. At the time, Ricky, her husband, went on about how Poppy had run off with another man. Not everyone believed the story, and Ryan Houseman, Poppy's lover, was one of them. He was distraught when Poppy left.

They'd been high school sweethearts, but when Poppy found out Ryan's previous girlfriend was pregnant with his baby, she left him and got married to Ricky. The rest was history. For months, people were sorry for Ricky because Poppy left him, so when he took up with Melanie Bailey, everyone was happy to see him pick his life back up and go on. Soon after, Ricky went around saying Poppy signed the divorce papers and he was marrying Melanie. The gossip fervor died down and no one brought it up again. That is, until now.

He'd been working at Pineville at the time. The Sheriff, Harry Dalby, was within a year of retirement and Harry had passed away since then. Something about that body showing up so close to the Turner house, well, it didn't add up. With the eraser end of his pencil, Zeb tapped his forehead trying to work out the story line regarding Poppy, Ricky, Melanie, and, of course, Ryan Houseman.

Putting down the pencil, he took a drink of his coffee. Good police work meant knowing when to separate the facts from the fiction. The truth was, Poppy Turner Mitchell needed to be looked up and the best place to begin was with Ricky and Ryan, her former husband and lover.

Zeb sighed. He didn't enjoy going over to the Mitchell residence. Melanie always did the flirty vixen routine with him, while Ricky got defensive and acted like a puffed-up horse's back end.

Picking up his hat, his holster, and his gun, Zeb told the officer at the front desk he was headed over to Mitchell's Fertilizer Farm and to get a message to Deputy Kirchner to contact both dentists in town when he was done with the alien situation.

Within ten minutes, Zeb was driving down the road to the opposite side of town from The Whispering Pines RV Park. He didn't relish this visit. Only yesterday, he'd been on the phone with Ricky about the old Turner house burning down. Ricky had been pugnacious and querulous, saying that the Sheriff's department must be letting thieves and pyromaniacs run free on the streets of Willow Valley.

Asking Ricky where his ex-wife was currently residing made the Sheriff chuckle to himself. He imagined the banty rooster of a man huffing and pawing at the ground after that question. Thinking about what went on at Mitchell's Fertilizer Farm and his own eminent task of visiting with Ricky and Melanie, Zeb realized both were dirty jobs, but someone had to do them.

Scene Break

Deputy Kirchner was finishing up his task of talking with Mrs. Townsend. He'd been forced to spend over an hour and a half following her from one corner of the house to another, being shown places she was convinced someone hid and spied on her. The patient deputy explained to her that most likely it wasn't alien life watching her through the windows. She took his attempt at a sane explanation as a direct insult and that's when the not-so-pleasant visit took a decided downturn. With an indignant stamp of her foot, Mrs. Townsend declared that she was dead certain something or someone had been fiddling with her things, making faces at her in mirrors, puffing air at the top of her head, and that unseen eyes followed her through her house.

Kirchner stifled a grin at the comment about scary faces in the mirrors. Sheriff Walker wanted all his officers always to perform their jobs with great respect for the public. With that in mind, the deputy didn't let the thought of Mrs. Townsend's overly powdered face or her dyed, flaming-red hair and cobalt blue-shadowed eyelids sink too deeply into his brain for fear his true feelings would be written all over his face.

"You may have some kids messing about your place, Mrs. Townsend," Deputy Kirchner said soothingly. "Have you considered a security alarm and maybe some well-placed cameras?"

The petite yet severe-looking woman peered up at him with an intense, wasp-like gaze. "Yes, I like that idea, Deputy. I'll invest in a system and when I have proof of their games, I expect your office to prosecute the ruffians to the full extent of the law or bring in the men in black if it's an alien."

A quick burst of laughter tried to explode from Kirchner's mouth, but with great control, he immediately suppressed it and forced a cough instead in a respectful attempt to cover his momentary slip in professionalism.

"Of course, ma'am, give us a call if anything causes you concern and especially if you catch someone prowling about the place."

Kirchner stepped out of the front door and tipped his hat at the two beady eyes glaring up at him from the barely opened, cracked door.

"Have a good day, ma'am," he scarcely was able to say before the door was shut and the sound of locks were heard being secured.

Once back at his police vehicle, he checked the messages on his laptop. Sheriff Walker needed him to contact both of the dental offices operating within the time frame of the woman's murder. It was likely this investigation would need to be expanded to include the wider regional area, if not the state and beyond. They simply didn't have any missing persons within their jurisdiction from which to pick. He knew the two dentists to call, so with a quick internet reference for their numbers, he dialed Dr. Dempster, the same dentist he'd gone to as a kid.

The receptionist answered the phone.

"Dr. Dempster's office, Laney speaking. How may I help you?"

Deputy Kirchner thought he recognized the winsome voice of a girl he'd gone to high school with only a few years ago.

"Laney? Laney Bodwell, is that you?" Kirchner asked in a friendly, upbeat way.

"Sure is. Who's this?"

"Tommy Kirchner," he responded, the excitement evident in his voice.

"Tommy!" she exclaimed. "I saw your picture in the paper a few months ago. You looked so handsome in your uniform."

Her tone was warm and flirty. Kirchner's heart took a leap into his throat. He'd had a huge crush on Laney Bodwell all four years of high school. Long, auburn hair and dark eyes, he'd lost his bearings every time he'd tried to ask her out back then. Even now, his mouth went dry, but he had a job to do, so he pushed on.

"Laney, I've got an investigation into a missing person and wondered if Dr. Dempster would be able to help us out?"

"Sure," she answered, drawing out the word into two syllables.

Encouraged, Tommy quickly tried to finagle an opportunity to go by the dentist's office.

"Would it be okay if I came by and left some paperwork with you and talked with Dr. Dempster?"

"May I put you on hold for a minute, Tommy?" Laney asked sweetly.

"Sure, I'll wait."

His mind was doing all sorts of nervous calculations, none of which had anything to do with the actual investigation. Would she still look like she did in high school? What if she had a boyfriend? She might even be married. The last thought put a real damper on his high hopes.

Her voice came back on the line. "Tommy, you can come over. I've asked Dr. D. if he had some time to see you and he's happy to help in any way he can. If you would be here about four o'clock, he's sure to have some time to talk."

"Thanks, Laney. I'll be there."

Deputy Kirchner ended his call and, for a minute or two, stared out the windshield of his police vehicle. His mind snapped back to his morning coffee with Mrs. Caruthers. What was it she'd said about someone with a gentle soul coming into his life soon? Was she right? Kirchner quickly shook the idea of Mrs. Caruthers being able to foresee the future out of his head. That psychic stuff was good timing or character reading. Wasn't it?

But even a hardened cynic, will have his moments of doubt when hope blows a mistral wind whispering promises of love. A freeing leap of faith was the small thing being asked, so Tommy grinned broadly, checked his reflection in the rearview mirror and kept his fingers crossed about his visit to Dr. Dempster's.

Chapter 14

Out Highway 59, the landscape became rolling pastures, a few farmhouses scattered about, and the occasional bridge spanning clear-flowing creeks. Mainly rural, with the parcels of land being between fifty and a hundred acres, this neck-of-the-woods summed up southern Missouri.

The families who owned these farms knew each other well, protected each other's property, and helped out with the emergencies of farm life such as broken fences and wandering cow herds until everyone worked together to get them back in their rightful pasture.

Zeb understood the customs and manners of these farmers simply because he was one of them, but people like Ricky and Melanie were different. They were the kind of people who always made you feel like you owed them something or they were quick to point out the things they thought you weren't doing right.

The Mitchells always had either a sneer or a look on their face like something smelled bad. But, Zeb thought to himself, things usually did smell pretty bad at Mitchell Farm, mainly like chicken and pig manure.

The dirt road down to their farm was rough and full of potholes. Wafting up in the heat of the day was the pungent aroma of fresh manure. Zeb saw the old ranch style house come into view. The grass in the yard was high and looked like they hadn't bothered to mow it in weeks. No flowers of any kind were in evidence anywhere and one window screen sagged out of the casement giving the eyes of the house a sadness to their expression. One depressed dog was chained to a post, and when Zeb stopped his car, the poor dog lifted her head and let her tail beat out a sullen welcome.

It didn't take long for Ricky to appear in the front door. His shirt was half-tucked into his pants, and, as usual, there was a smug look on the pudgy face. Flies swarmed the front porch where Zeb saw the remnants of what must have been the dog's meals simply slopped down on the concrete for the animal to consume. No water dish anywhere.

"Come over to tell me ya caught the bastard who burned down my house?" Ricky sneered, still standing in the frame of his front door.

"Nope, but I did come by to ask you if you have Poppy's address or contact information."

The bomb of a question just hung in the heat of the fly-filled front yard. Zeb never took his eyes from Ricky's swollen face. The bloated, fleshy cheeks quivered ever so slightly, and he gripped the handle of the door in an effort to surreptitiously steady himself.

"I don't have it."

"You don't have any idea where your ex-wife is living? Don't you have to pay her some sort of support?"

Ricky rallied with the last question. "She's the one who

ran off! I didn't owe her nothin! Poppy's gone and I don't give a crap where she is."

At the mention of Poppy, another voice sounded somewhere from the depths of the house. Soon, Melanie made her appearance. Wearing a purple tube top stretched across her corpulent bosom and tight work-out pants, she pushed through the door past Ricky saying in a cooingly sweet tone, "Did I hear you mention Poppy?"

The real grist of the experience was about to begin. Zeb waited for it.

"Get some clothes on, Melanie," Ricky barked.

"These are clothes!" she shrieked. "I gotta right to wear whatever I want."

"You're not decent!" he yelled, getting red in the face. His blubbery lips protruded even more with his heated rage.

Melanie turned her 'Real Wives of Poultry County' persona off and turned to Zeb, completely ignoring Ricky, and asked, "Zeb, did I hear you say something about Poppy?"

"I'm here to let you know we've found a body in a pit down at The Whispering Pines RV Park. It's a woman of about thirty years of age."

Zeb let the announcement sink in and continued, "I need Poppy's contact information, and I thought Ricky might have it."

Melanie's eyes became like cold steel. She straightened up, losing her typical pelvic forward posture and said, "Why don't you go ask Ryan Houseman? He should have it. We don't want any contact with her."

"So, you don't know where she is?" Zeb pushed one more time. "Do you know how I might get a hold of her mother?"

"No," came the hard, firm reply from Melanie's thin-lipped, overly made-up, crimson mouth. "Poppy's mother's left, and she hasn't been back since."

Zeb walked over to where the dog lay and reached down to unhook the chain from the post. The dog's tail thumped against the grass.

"What you doin with my dog?" Ricky bellowed from his fouled front steps.

"I'm taking this dog with me," Zeb replied in an even, cool voice.

"That's my dog!" Ricky roared indignantly.

"Not anymore, it isn't. I'm also fining you two hundred dollars for animal cruelty. My deputies will be out here after thirty days, Ricky, if you haven't come in and paid your fine. No more pets for you for five years. If you're caught with one on your property, I'll see to it you serve time. Understand?"

Ricky and Melanie glared and slammed the front door. Zeb was relieved to be free of their company.

"Come on, girl. I know just the person for you."

In less than five minutes, man and dog were making their way back to Willow Valley. A Conway Twitty song was playing on the radio, windows were down to receive the fresh springtime air and one free, happy dog was catching the breeze, tongue out and ears flapping joyfully in the wind.

Scene break

Sonya was excited to be hosting her first séance since she'd hung her shingle out to the Willow Valley community. Flowers had been brought in from her garden and thoughtfully arranged in two different vases, one for the polished cherry wood dining table and another for the glass coffee table in the living room. For a while, Willard followed her from one room to the other until he appeared to tire of her over-activity and lay down on the cushy floor pillow under the black baby grand piano.

The lemon cream pie was chilling nicely in the vintage Frigidaire and Frank Sinatra was crooning from the record player. White, lace curtains caught the cool breeze and billowed drowsily as Willard's eyelids drooped and finally closed. A soft snoring sound mixed with the dreamy music of Count Basie's Orchestra, which ably supported the Chairman of the Board's rendition of 'Fly Me to the Moon' that played on the old Victrola.

Sonya swept around the room, doing a few dance steps while she used her feather duster on the furniture. It was fun to know she was going to have people in the house. Everything was ready for her guests to arrive. She'd laid out coffee cups, saucers, spoons, cream and sugar, and a stack of pretty china plates with tiny rosebuds painted around their rims for her guests to use when the pie was served.

As she considered the chinaware, it occurred to her that maybe she'd gotten carried away. It was a séance, not a meet and greet. With sudden insight, she realized it was actually both, so with a toss of the feather duster into the slim closet in the laundry room, Sonya finished with her tidying up. Her timing was perfect because the doorbell rang, and Willard beat a quick line from his spot under the piano to the entrance alcove, barking and joyfully announcing they had company.

Sonya peeked out of the kitchen to see who was at her front door. It was Mr. Pepper. She took off her apron, throwing it across a bar stool and quickly went through the house. Swinging the door open, she said, "Hello, Mr. Pepper. How are you?"

There, in what must have been his best suit and carrying a handpicked bouquet of wild flowers, was a polished and well turned-out gentleman coming to call.

"Good afternoon, Mrs. Caruthers," he said, his smile reaching from ear to ear and his eyes twinkling with excitement. "I know I'm early, but I wanted to talk with you…privately." He stretched out the hand holding the flowers toward her in a heartfelt gesture and said, "These are for you."

"Oh, they are lovely, Mr. Pepper," Sonya said warmly. "Please do come in." She stepped aside to allow him entrance, and he waited politely until she showed him into the living room.

"Please make yourself comfortable. If you wouldn't mind, I will add your beautiful flowers to the ones I've already picked and put in this vase. Is that okay with you?" she asked solicitously.

"Please do," he said with eager courtesy. "I think they

will go together nicely."

After the flowers were reorganized and it was agreed that the new arrangement was even better than the first, Sonya offered Mr. Pepper some refreshment. He readily accepted. Within a short time, they were comfortably sitting down with two cups of hot coffee and a plate of shortbread cookies. Mr. Pepper finally had an opportunity to explain why he needed an early visit.

"I've been giving some thought to what happened yesterday morning. At the time of the incident, I was too upset to remember details, but since then, something has come back to me." He gave Sonya a wary look as if unsure if he should proceed.

"Please continue. This may be of some help to me, Mr. Pepper, especially if we are going to try and contact our ghost tonight," Sonya said encouragingly.

"Well, I'm not sure I want to be a part of the séance, Mrs. Caruthers. In fact, I don't know how my pastor would feel about us communing with spirits. I thought it might be helpful for you," he gave her a shy smile, "if you knew that I heard a name called out yesterday morning and it wasn't one I recognized."

Sonya was excited, but also, a bit affected by Mr. Pepper's worry regarding 'communing with spirits'. Taking a needed moment to think by sipping her coffee, she offered a compromise.

"Mr. Pepper, I do understand how you feel about the séance. It is fine if you prefer not to be here. You know your comfort zone and I wouldn't want to create conflict for anyone regarding their faith. I would be so grateful if you would share what you remember hearing yesterday, though."

This response of Sonya's had the desired effect. Mr. Pepper appeared to relax considerably. He took a deep breath and said, "Monkeyface."

Taken aback, Sonya said, "What?"

"Monkey face," Mr. Pepper repeated. "The spirit, if you will, said Monkey face."

"Oh!" Sonya said, much relieved, and leaned back in her seat. For a second, she thought Mr. Pepper had been calling her that. "I believe that must be a term of endearment, Mr. Pepper. Did your wife ever use it?"

"Definitely not, I don't like monkeys."

"Hmmm," Sonya mused for a second or two. "This may be a wonderful clue. I'll bring it up tonight at our…spirit therapy session."

Mr. Pepper smiled with a knowing twinkle in his eyes. "Mrs. Caruthers, it's kind of you to try and sugarcoat it. I wanted to let you know I'm going back to New Jersey to be with my daughter." He paused as if he wanted to say more but was unsure how to proceed.

"Mr. Pepper? Is there something bothering you?" Sonya asked.

He turned to face her directly. "Mrs. Caruthers, would you do me the honor of coming with me to my lodge's dance this Friday next?" His face was a mixture of hope and fear.

Sonya didn't hesitate. "I would love to come with you, Mr. Pepper. I adore dancing, but I'll have to warn you, I've got two left feet."

Mr. Pepper practically glowed with happiness. "Thank you so much, Mrs. Caruthers. I promise it will be a fun time."

"It's Sonya. Please call me Sonya, Mr. Pepper."

"Yes, thank you and, if you will, please call me Saul," he returned.

"Great! We have a date then, Saul."

They both smiled and Mr. Pepper stood up.

"I must be going. I hope you won't think badly of me for not staying for your séance this evening."

"Absolutely not, Saul. I understand perfectly, and if we're successful this evening, the residents of The Whispering Pines RV Park may sleep undisturbed in their beds for many years to come."

Sonya saw Mr. Pepper out through the front gate and waved as he drove away. It was getting late. The sun was still well above the far hills. She climbed her front steps and went inside as the evening bugs sang their song.

Flipping on her outside lights, she hoped the path to her door would be easier for her guests to traverse with a porch light to guide them and yard lights to keep them from tripping over the pavers. Even though its source may be diverse in nature, a light that is true will always lead you to a good destination.

Chapter 15

It occurred to Deputy Kirchner as he parked the police vehicle in front of Dr. Dempster's office that he'd not been to the dentist in about five years. He hoped Laney wouldn't ask him because it would look like he didn't take proper care of his teeth, which might be a turn-off. With a quick inspection of his smile, he took at deep, centering breath of air and let it out slowly. He was ready.

The reception area was exactly the same as it had been when his mother brought him here. As he quickly scanned the room, he recognized the same posters of a dancing tooth with a huge toothy smile and the caption which read at the top, 'Mr. Smiley Brushed Twice a Day' and 'You Should, TOO'. This was reassuring because he definitely brushed twice a day. With more confidence, he scanned the room for signs of the beautiful Laney.

Tommy saw the top of a head behind the tall reception desk. The pretty auburn hair was pulled up into a bun with a pencil pushed through it. It must be her. His heart did a double beat. He walked up with a friendly, yet manly policeman strut and looked down at the top of the head. What he saw next made him cringe noticeably. The woman sitting at the desk had a beard. Rocked by the horror of Laney with a beard, he couldn't focus anymore on the face that was lifting up to greet him.

"How may I help you?" she asked nicely.

"Laney?" his voice in his ears sounded croaky and hollow.

"God, no!" the woman said with a bemused laugh. "I'm Percy. Laney had to step out for an hour. Her dog was seen running down Elm Street. He must have gotten loose."

In a flash, Deputy Kirchner realized it was a man behind the desk with his hair in a bun and bits of weird jewelry dangling off him. He laughed a bit too heartily and said, "Thank you. I need to see Dr. Dempster for a moment."

"Have a seat and I'll let him know you're here."

Percy, the desk person, got up from his seat revealing his lanky frame decked out in scrubs with different cartoon characters on them. His man-bun had two pieces of hair jewelry clipped into it, an enameled dragonfly and a pencil with an eraser in the shape of a skull and crossbones. He disappeared through one of the doors, leaving Tommy to find a seat and wonder at how men's fashion became more confusing every day.

"Come on back, Officer Kirchner," Percy said from the door that led to the back rooms. "Doc will see you now." As Tommy passed by him, Percy grabbed him by the arm and said in a low whisper, "Be ready, he says he's going to take a look in your mouth. He says you haven't been in for a while." Percy raised his eyebrows in a gesture of mock horror. "He does this to everyone who was at one time a child patient and hasn't been back since their mama quit making their appointments."

Kirchner, a bit disappointed by not seeing Laney, but also relieved the hairy-faced person was someone else, followed Percy obediently to a bright, well-equipped examination room.

"Have a seat." Percy pointed to the chair.

"Umm, I don't think I have time for this today."

The Deputy's attempt to excuse himself was quickly snuffed out. Percy put one hand on his hip and, with an extremely affronted divaesque finger wave, mouthed the words, "Really?" Pointing to the seat firmly, he said in a low, no-nonsense tone, "Don't try my last nerve. That man is driving me crazy. If he wants to look at your teeth, for the love of God, let him."

Percy pursed his lips and lowered his eyelids. He never lost eye contact continuing to point at the chair. Once Kirchner finally relented and dutifully sat down, Percy muttered a bit under his breath about how put out he was and put a paper napkin bib covered with cartoon animals around Tommy's neck. The manly deputy looked down to see lions, puppies, and even a crocodile smiling up at him with captions saying things like 'eat fruits and vegetables,' 'brush and floss every day,' and 'see the dentist twice a year.' Tommy thought to himself those were odd things for meat eaters to say.

"The doctor will be in soon," Percy said, whisking out of the room in what appeared to be an exasperated huff. The Deputy sat staring mutely at another poster. This one showed a toothpaste tube drawn to look like a rocket with a caption that read, 'Take Off for a Beautiful Smile'. It had a cartoon cat dressed like an astronaut sitting astride the tube while waving out at the viewer. There were, at least, twenty pictures hand-drawn by kids taped to the examination room's walls. He recognized the name of one of his coworkers' kids. Deputy Kirchner hoped that no one he knew would walk in and see him wearing the kiddy bib. This was the kind of stuff the other officers lived for.

"Well, well, well, Mr. Kirchner or should I say Officer Kirchner?" Dr. Dempster smiled waggishly from the doorway. "Haven't seen you in some time. How're your mother and father?" The dentist of Tommy's childhood hadn't changed much. He was fit from playing golf three times a week, his hair was a little grayer, and his iconic bowtie was neatly tied around his neck. Today the tie's fabric had golf clubs, golf balls, and golf carts.

"They're doing fine, sir. I came here to ask you…" but Tommy didn't get a chance to finish. Dr. Dempster had already moved behind him and flipped on the overhead light. With a steel dental tool, he explored Tommy's back molars.

"Sorry, son, but I see your flossing is lacking in merit. When was your last cleaning?"

Tommy tried to answer, but as anyone knows, it's impossible to answer other than an 'iglick kna' which was an attempt at 'I don't know.'

"We'll set you up with Laney. She does an excellent job. Can't get you in for about four months. You definitely need some work done in here."

Dr. Dempster wagged his head back and forth in a show of displeasure at Tommy's lack of good oral hygiene care.

He touched a tooth toward the back making Tommy jump and let out an, "Ow!"

"Ah ha! You have a cavity. That's not good. We'd better get you in before four months. I'll try and work you in. Your parents did a good job taking care of your teeth Tommy, so don't let all their good efforts go by the wayside."

Finished with his examination and the lecture, Dr. Dempster pushed away from the chair and raised it back to a normal position.

"Okay, tell me what you're really in here for," he said taking the paper bib from Tommy's neck. He went around to another chair and sat down crossing his long skinny legs revealing bright blue socks with a variety of waterfowl on them.

"We have a female body found in a grave not far from here, over at The Whispering Pines RV Park. Female, probably around twenty-five to thirty years of age and she's been in the ground for around a year. County forensics is doing a DNA sequence test on the teeth, which means we'll need to check those results against files of women who went missing around that time. We'd like to have your help with your patient files."

"Absolutely, you can work with Laney on this. She's the one who runs my office. When will you need to see her?"

"We have to wait on County, but the reports should be in tomorrow." In an effort to gain some information, Tommy turned the conversation around to the topic of Laney. "I went to high school with Laney Bodwell. Haven't seen her in a while. It'll be nice to catch up again."

Dr. Dempster gave the young man a slow smile and his expression hardened. No humor was behind his eyes as his eyebrows came together catching Tommy in their pincher-like union. "She's still a nice-looking young lady, Kirchner, but I'll say to you what I say to all the young bucks who come nosing around. If you're planning anything unworthy of such a sweet young woman, you'd better look elsewhere. She's been hurt by her worthless ex-husband enough for any woman's lifetime, so unless you plan on being a decent man before, during and after the wooing, go on down the road and stay clear."

Tommy appreciated the Doc's papa bear threat. He was also relieved to hear that Laney obviously hadn't changed much since high school.

"I didn't mean anything disrespectful, sir. I remember her from when we went to school together. She was, well, to be honest, the most beautiful girl I ever saw. Sorry to hear she had a rough time during her marriage."

"He was a no-good, philandering piece of human trash, but she loved him. It never ceases to amaze me how some women's nature for nurturing can work against them when it comes to the men they pick and the children they rear. That's why I've made it my job to make sure the worthless types don't get a toehold."

Tommy stood up and held out his hand for the Doc to shake in a gesture of understanding between two men. The older man looked up at the younger, raised his hand and shook the offered one.

"Don't worry, Dr. Dempster. If I misbehaved to a

woman, my dad would kill me long before you ever laid a hand on me and what was left of my hide, my mother would go to work on."

"Good! You've been raised right. In that case, Laney won't be around today. Had to go look for her dog. Call her tomorrow and set up a time to visit. Here's a new toothbrush and some floss. Get to work on that mouth, son. Women like to see a man with pearly whites."

Deputy Kirchner said his goodbyes and breathed a sigh of relief once he'd exited the dentist's office. Old Doc Dempster wasn't messing around about Laney or about better brushing. That was the blessing or the curse, depending on your outlook, of living in a small town. Everyone knew your business, knew your parents, and was willing to give you a good firm boot in the backend whenever you needed it and usually with your family's blessing.

Chapter 16

Eight o'clock finally arrived. The weather decided to play along. Gentle rumblings of thunder were heard moving closer from the west. The sun had long since settled, and the earlier warmth it provided had been blown away with the oncoming storm.

A short, round bus with a brightly emblazoned 'The Whispering Pines RV Park' along its sides, pulled up to Sonya's warmly lit two-story Victorian cottage.

The first two visitors to de-board were Lewis and Clark, and they did so with a great rush. Extremely excited by their ride on the bus, they planted their noses to the ground, drinking in the hundreds of new smells the town offered to their gifted noses.

"Boys!" Marnie called with a hint of frantic in her tone. The two eager beagles had jumped train before she'd had a chance to corral them and put on their leashes. "Sit! Stay! Oh for God's sake, Noah, let me through. The dogs are going to follow their noses to Timbuktu before I get off this carnival ride."

It had been a carnival ride in every sense of the metaphor. Noah had complained the entire ride about dog hair floating willy-nilly on currents from the air conditioning and used his personal lint brush continuously. Lewis and Clark slipped their chair restraints and ran blissfully up and down the aisle making a ruckus at one point over an old soda can they found under a seat in the back, while Marnie shouted for someone to grab them. Julia made an effort to talk over the dog-versus-can commotion about her last trip to Branson, Missouri, where she'd seen a live tribute show with singer-actors like Elvis Presley, Patsy Cline, The Blues Brothers, and Buddy Holly. Her greatest moment in life had been getting all their autographs. No one was willing to point out that the signatures were utterly bogus.

Dale, Marnie's handyman at The Whispering Pines, threatened to give his resignation at the disorderliness of the beagles' behavior. As for Marnie, she was right on the edge of accepting if it. The bus ride proved the dogs were in need of better training, but Dale was driving her nuts with his constant grumping about them.

"I told you those dogs of yours would run off on you one day," Dale called as she ran down the sidewalk after Lewis and Clark.

"Is this the time, Dale, to start with the 'I told you so stuff'? Help me!" Marnie yelled back.

Dale put two fingers up to his mouth and whistled sharply, halting Lewis and Clark's great discovery-filled adventure. "Come here!" he commanded. The two wayward beagles trotted back toward The Whispering Pines' bus and waited patiently until Marnie got their leashes on them. Once the boys were secured, Dale looked around Pickwick Street and gave it a good once over with his critical eyes.

"My Aunt Martha lived not far from here when I was a boy. Loved her raspberry tarts. Needs some paint on the eaves though and that hydrangea bush looks like it could use some proper fertilizer."

Marnie gave her handyman a sour look. "Dale, I'm going to offer your good services to Mrs. Caruthers. I'm sure she'd love your never-ending excellent advice and a willing hand to help her around here."

Dale did the hands in the front-pants-pockets gesture and the scrunching up of his mouth like he'd tasted something bitter and said, "Just saying, Marnie. No need to get yourself in a dither."

Sonya opened her front door. "Hello! Please come in. Marnie, bring Lewis and Clark through so the dogs can do their greetings first." She let Willard run past her to where his guests were waiting, their excitement evident by the wiggling of bodies. "Please, everyone come this way."

Sonya's house practically glowed with anticipation of its guests. Lamps created warm pools of soft light giving the room a cozy feel. The wood-beamed ceilings, flowers, and the lace-covered dining table with its yummy offerings of pie, shortbread cookies, and plenty of coffee and tea, imbued the new arrivals with a sense of timeless gentility and pleasant expectation.

"Please, help yourselves," Sonya said with a twinkle in her eye and good cheer in her voice. Everyone, including the furry guests, talked much as people will do when they find themselves among good company and delicious food. The three dogs were given their treats and they soon found their way back outside for a good deal of nosing about and maybe some running games. The humans, once settled with warm drinks and their own plates filled with edible delights, discussed the events leading up to this evening's 'spirit therapy session.'

"Do you think we will make contact with the ghost?" Julia said, her eyes full of hope followed by a touch of anxiety.

"Absolutely, we will," Sonya said. "I hope she can tell us something about herself and she's strong enough to show us what she needs."

Dale put his hefty slice of lemon pie down on the table beside his chair and said, "Mrs. Caruthers, would you be a good sport and let me inspect this room for strings, speakers, and any other instruments? I'm not a believer in this type of chicanery and want some insurance we're not being played for a bunch of dimwitted fools."

"Dale! How absolutely rude," Marnie blurted, the expression on her face one of horror at his lack of delicacy.

"Oh, not to worry, Marnie. I think Mr. Smith is correct in asking. If I were going to someone's house for something as unusual as a séance, I mean a spirit therapy session, I'd want some proof as well." Sonya stood up and invited Dale to go anywhere he wished, opening doors, drawers, and looking under furniture.

"Treat it like your own home, Mr. Smith, and when you're done come back to let us know what you've learned," Sonya said.

"He'll probably come back and give you a critique on

you housekeeping, Sonya. He's a mess, but as honest as the day is long," Marnie said with a laugh. "This pie is incredible. I'd love the recipe."

Julia and Noah were talking quietly among themselves, and Sonya had taken Marnie to the kitchen for the recipe when Dale wondered up from the basement.

"I've done a clean sweep, Mrs. Caruthers, and there's nothing cattywampus about your place. I did see a dryer vent issue in your utility room. The plastic tie isn't as secure as it should be around the outflow tube. I could fix that if you'd like."

Sonya and Marnie gave Dale a slightly perplexed but good-humored look. "Don't worry with that tonight, Mr. Smith, I'll see to it tomorrow. Thank you, though, for your inspection and suggestion."

The three of them went back into the living room and Sonya asked everyone to pull their chairs together around the coffee table. Julia and Noah stayed comfortably ensconced on the sofa with Julia scooting closer to him saying with a schoolgirl's excitement, "You don't mind do you, Noah? I'm a little scared."

"Of course not, Julia, I'll protect you," Noah said with obvious delight in his voice at Julia's flattering endorsement of his manliness.

Sonya turned most of the lamps off in the room. The dogs came in and settled themselves. They were ready to rest after their play in the garden. With everything quiet, Sonya sat down, took a deep breath, and relaxed. All eyes were on her, but no one said a word. There was a tingling of expectation in the air. Sonya put out a mental push searching the spiritual atmosphere for hints of energy once a part of our physical world but now separate.

The wind picked up outside. A soft pattering of rain against the windows diverted attention for a moment, but soon all were aware of a low murmuring sound coming from the air molecules in the room. As it grew in loudness, it took on a theatrical quality. The moaning crescendoed to an ear-splitting decibel, more as if for effect than for the actual misery of the moaner. Sonya's brow furrowed. The entity who was beginning to energize the room wasn't the one she expected, but she wasn't surprised. His love for theatrics and a willing audience had brought Fritz at top speed back from his ancestral duties in the Highlands. The dogs barked and growled at the ceiling.

Noah, Julia, Marnie, and Dale sat looking slightly pale and horror-stricken. No one moved, but Sonya was sure one of them would bolt soon. She needed to bring Fritz to heel and fast.

"Show yourself, spirit," she commanded, knowing Fritz wouldn't materialize. There was a pause in the moaning while Fritz considered Sonya's bluff. Lights rattled, doors opened and slammed shut, making everyone jump to their feet. The dogs went crazy and a great uproar of masculine laughter boomed through the house. Fritz was having a wonderful time.

Dale yelled, "Get thee behind me, Satan!" which had the effect of encouraging the rascally Fritz further. He flipped the hat Dale was wearing up into Sonya's chandelier and pinched Julia on the rump, causing her to practically fling herself into Noah's more than willing arms.

"Fritz! Stop this right now!" Sonya yelled, her face turning a smidgen red. "This is a serious attempt at contacting a ghost who's in distress and you're not being funny."

"On the contrary, Sonya," Fritz laughed from the rafters, "I'm tickled to death!"

"What's going on Sonya?" Marnie asked nervously. She and the others had stood up and were near the vestibule.

Sonya tried to compose herself. She took a deep breath and said, "This is going to be hard to believe for some of you but I have a ghost for a friend," Sonya said. "He likes to play jokes sometimes."

If he hadn't been already dead, Sonya wanted to take a shot at Fritz herself. "He'll be good," she said as she looked at the ceiling, "Won't you? If you don't, I'll put this entire house off-limits to you, and you know I can do it."

The sound of someone making a loud razzberry was piped through the house. Everyone waited nervously near the front door vestibule.

Sonya said, "Fritz, if you want to be of some help, please try and bring the lost ghost to us. Your help would be much appreciated."

A sullen response in a low murmur was heard. "I'll try, but what a bunch of nervous nellies. Give me a few minutes."

"Please, everyone, I know this may feel extremely strange, but if you'll give me a few minutes to explain, I'm sure it will make sense."

The entire group came back to the sitting area and composed themselves. Marnie called the dogs over to the front door and let them out. She put the yard lights on and told the boys to be good.

"You see," Sonya said, "a few years ago on a trip to Canada, I met Fritz, a ghost, who became my friend. The thing to understand about any ghost is that they're still people and some refuse to travel on to their next level of existence. There may be many reasons for this, and in Fritz's case, it's because he's extremely attached to his home in Scotland. Ghosts, like living people, want to have personal friendships, travel, feel like they have a safe place to dwell and enjoy amusements. Fritz loves being a troublemaker, but he's harmless, and most days, he's a good friend."

Sonya took in the perplexed expressions of her guests. She pushed forward. "It can be an asset to have a ghost who is attached to a living person. They try to help where they can if they are a decent sort to begin with. I believe Fritz has a better chance of bringing the ghost who's haunting The Whispering Pines to us than even I do. He'll try and to get her to come to us, and if she doesn't know she's dead yet, then having another entity who's capable of keeping up with her is a more efficient means of communication and delivery."

"So, why didn't you use this Fritz person yesterday and save me from being nearly scared to death this morning by a crazy she-ghost?" Noah complained sourly.

"Ghosts can be extremely undependable, and Fritz is no exception. I did ask him, but he was being mischievous and difficult at the time, so he didn't help. Presently, he's more open to being useful because he needs to make it up to me. Also, if he doesn't play nice, I'm going to block him from the house for a month."

"You're a witch," Dale said with a firm nod of his head. "I'm going to go sit in the car, Marnie. She's got dealings with the Devil, you can be sure of it."

"Dale," Marnie said like a mother who was on her last nerve, "she's a medium and a spirit therapist. Try to keep your mind from slamming shut every time something new presents itself to your extremely limited worldview. If you want to sit in the bus like a scaredy-cat, fine, but it's not a flattering image of how a true military man would handle himself."

Goaded by the military man comment, Dale made one last stab at his moral outrage. "It's the principle of the matter. I don't want to dabble in the occult. That woman will bring trouble on herself and us if we don't leave."

"You're a bore, old man," said a voice from the air. Fritz was back. "Sit down and shut up!" he boomed. "I'm as good a Presbyterian as you ever hope to be, and the chapel I personally paid for in my village is one of the finest in all of Scotland. Devil, schmevil! If you want to see something truly evil, look at your own dull wit."

Dale sat dumbstruck. He clamped his mouth shut and appeared to seethe at being insulted by an invisible ghost.

Sonya took the opportunity to bring everyone back to the real matter at hand. "Did you find the ghost, Fritz?"

"She's here. A bit daffy and clingy, but she's here,

nonetheless," Fritz said in a bored tone.

Motioning for everyone to please take their seats as quickly as possible, Sonya grabbed the reins of the situation.

"Will you give us your name?" she asked in a firm yet kind tone.

"My name is Poppy Turner." As soon as she uttered her name, the ghost sobbed. No one saw the spirit, but on the grand piano, the flowers Sonya and Mr. Pepper had arranged were fidgeting about in the vase like someone was blowing directly on them.

"Will you tell us what happened to you?"

The ghost let out a wail making Julia practically jump onto Noah's lap again. So far, Sonya's spiritual therapy session was working beautifully in Noah's favor, but it was Fritz who shored up the situation with a commanding, "Get on with it woman! Tell my lady what or who done you in!"

Everyone in the room sat stock still not daring to move. Even though Fritz was almost two hundred years dead, he was a force to be reckoned with when it came to ordering people about. To be fair, it came naturally to him.

The weepy ghost added a few sniffles and finally answered. "I don't know how I died. I woke up at the bottom of the stairs." She was quiet for a moment and added. "Someone pushed me."

Sonya jumped in at the last comment not wishing for Poppy to lose her momentum in her story.

"Do you remember what was happening before you were pushed?" she asked.

"Ricky and I were having an argument and he stormed out of the house." The ghost of Poppy cried again, "I miss Monkey Face! Where is Ryan?"

Everyone in the room exchanged furtive expressions. Dale, unfortunately, was the one who didn't stay mute.

"I knew it! I bet he killed her for the Turner Treasure. Where's the treasure, Poppy, and what ever happened to your Ma?"

Sonya quickly put her finger up to her lips at Dale's outburst, but it was too late. Poppy was on the move. She must have made a beeline for Dale believing he would know where to find her beloved Ryan. Doilies took flight and as the chilly presence of the spirit wafted past people, they gasped or jerked back in response to her touch. As Poppy plopped herself on top of Dale's lap, the terrified handyman looked as if he was in the grip of the Grim Reaper himself.

"Geeet it off of me!" he screamed sending the entire room into utter chaos as he got up and made a break for the front door.

People flung themselves out of their seats and scuttled to different corners of Sonya's pretty parlor. The people who stayed put were Sonya, Noah, and Julia. Even if Noah had wanted to run, he couldn't. Both of Julia's arms were wrapped around his neck, and she was sitting completely in his lap. To be sure, Noah was equally scared but unable to do much about it.

"Everyone settle down!" Sonya called out to her scurrying guests. "She thinks Dale knows where Ryan is. If you will all be calm, I will talk with her. Please come back

111

and we can finish this session."

Marnie, who was standing by the grand piano, went over and collected Dale. She dragged him back to his chair and promised him tomorrow would be a free day off if he'd sit down and be a man. Ashen-faced from his scare, he put his hand down near the space of the chair he was supposed to occupy to make sure that nothing else was already there.

"Poppy," Sonya asked, "what were you and Ricky, your husband, arguing about before you passed to the other side?"

Poppy didn't hesitate. "Money, Ricky wanted to know where the money was my family hid in the house. I don't know and I told him so. He was angry, and where is Ryan?"

Sonya knew what she had to do. Ghosts were lost without the ones they loved and Poppy needed to see Ryan again or, at least, know he was fine.

"Poppy, Ryan is still alive. He lives here in Willow Valley. If you will let me, I will make sure you see him, but you must promise to behave properly."

Nothing and no one moved in the room for a few brief seconds. Poppy's voice full of longing finally answered. "I understand."

"If Fritz comes back for you tomorrow, will you come again to this house if I promise to help you?" Sonya said with gentleness.

"Yes, but I don't want to go back to the house. It's so lonely and dark there." Poppy sniffled again.

"You don't have to go back, Poppy. Is there a special place you liked when you were alive? Remember, you must be respectful of living people," and with a look at Dale, she continued, "they're often scared by over-zealous ghostly attention."

"I like it here," came the weak reply.

"Stay with me then until you learn a few things, but don't scare my dog, Willard. He's already got Fritz to deal with, and that's enough for any terrier."

The energy that was Poppy faded from the room and soon no other unusual sounds were heard except the soft rolling thunder of the approaching storm.

"I think we're done here, everyone. I hope it hasn't been too much for any of you?" Sonya said raising herself up from her chair.

Her guests, a bit ashen in complexion, smiled weakly and began to rise. Having heard the sadness and loneliness in poor Poppy's voice, they'd found their hearts opening to the dead woman's plight. They each shook Sonya's hand and wished her a good night.

"I hope Poppy gets on with it," Dale said grudgingly. "I knew her and she was a beautiful woman. Sorry, to hear someone killed her."

Sonya smiled warmly at Dale's attempt at accepting a difficult new piece of understanding. "She's going to be fine. I hope she chooses to pass over soon. Murder victims do better when they go on to God. They truly need the healing more than others."

Dale smiled and patted Sonya on the shoulder. "Maybe you're not a heathen, Godless woman, after all."

Sonya burst out laughing good-naturedly. "I think you

meant that as a compliment, Mr. Smith, so I'm taking it that way."

"Call me Dale. It was one, and that's enough of the touchy feely stuff. I'm dead beat. Gotta get home and shake this mumbo jumbo stuff off."

Everyone piled back into the transport bus and waved goodbye. Sonya, feeling tired, made her way back up the front porch stairs and into the house. Locking the doors, she called for Willard and they soon were tucked into their soft beds. Right before she fell asleep, the spring thunderstorm broke over the distant hills and a soft rain tapped at her windows and pattered upon her roof. Perfect weather for a good night's rest and if she'd ever needed one, tonight was the night.

Chapter 17

Next morning, Willard woke up, did a deep stretch, and trotted downstairs while Sonya slept unawares in her fluffy bed. He liked to take care of his business followed by a reconnaissance run around the perimeter of his territory. The garden never disappointed in the early hours right after the sun rose. Wet grass, cool air, earthy smells and hungry, busy squirrels were the enticements Willard hoped would be waiting for him in his doggy garden paradise.

The boys, Lewis and Clark, made it clear to Willard last night that the body in the pit belonged to the ghost. They'd watched the ghost come out of the pit and followed it to a burnt out house. It was for Willard to figure out a way to let Sonya know this vital bit of information.

Pushing his body through the doggy door located off the back utility porch, he was met by the fresh, misty air of the morning, making him snort at its wetness while he sniffed at each spot along his habitual route.

That's when he heard it. The sound he'd come to loathe more than any other...the rasping, grating noise of four metal wheels rolling over the pavement along with one rubber-soled foot pounding the sidewalk in a rhythmic, drumming beat.

Willard went stiff. He turned his head, and his ears pricked up in an effort to focus all his canine senses on the approaching interloper. As if lifted from the sky above, his eager body took air and all four legs hit the ground at the same time springing him forward to the best spot along the garden fence to see The Boy on the Skateboard go by.

Out of the early morning fog, came Willard's nemesis like a puffing dragon on a gliding, silver foot-machine. The Boy blew out warm air from his lungs, which hung momentarily in the crisp air. With great self-control, Willard waited for the perfect time to unleash his first attack: a spirited volley of surprise barking. Hunkered down below an enormous snowball bush, he watched for the wheels to come perfectly in line with his vision. But something caused the noisy wheels to halt and fall completely silent.

Willard dared not move. He sniffed the air from his hiding spot and sure enough, he picked up The Boy's scent of cinnamon toast, wet sneakers, and hair gel. Somewhere, not more than ten feet from the garden's white picket fence, The Skateboard Devil waited, most likely aware of Willard's presence and feverish desire to set the score in his favor.

"Hey Willard, I know you're in there and I have a treat for you. Tastes real good," the boy baited.

Willard again let his nose test the particles on the air. He knew better than to move. The boy had tried this before and when Willard came out of his hiding spot, the spawn of evil had pretended to offer him a meat bone, but instead, quickly pelted him with eggs. Two baths later from the lady at the La Pooch Salon and with a demoralizing blue ribbon tied snuggly onto the top of his head, Willard wished for nothing more than to deal The Boy a worthy blow.

The air currents settled the smell of a spare rib bone wrapped in bacon onto Willard's olfactory nerves. If you're going to entice a dog you've already spurned once, you'd better go for the pinnacle of canine treats: pork.

"Maybe The Boy was good after all?" Willard thought to himself.

Dogs who've been treated well believe in the goodness of people. They give second, third, fourth and into infinity chances to humans. Willard's nose sniffed and his mouth watered at the bribe. Soon, his four feet moved without assistance and with bright eyes, he emerged from his safe spot.

"There you are," the boy said shooting glances around the garden and up at the windows of Sonya's house. "I brought you something. Do you want it?" He dangled the smoky treat at Willard. "Come on over here. I'll give you the whole thing."

Out of nowhere, the boy's skateboard stood up on its end and did a flashy twirl causing both Willard and his arch nemesis to turn their attention to the simple vehicle's unnatural trick.

"Hey! What's going on?" the boy said in a high-pitched voice, obviously unnerved by his skateboard's unusual exhibition. The bone he held limply in his sticky hand dropped to the ground and before Willard snatched it, it took flight again out into the brick-paved street and was lost down the storm sewer drain.

"You're a pestilence, and if I ever see you on this street again, I'll paint your face green, tie a tartan bow around your head, and make you dance a jig until your wee legs won't be able to push that wheeled horror for at least a fortnight!"

Upon hearing the cursing voice, the boy's mouth and eyes were about the same size, which meant all three were like round silver dollars. A blabber of nonsense gurgled from his dropped-jaw, and, like a cartoon character, he tried to take off from his spot on the sidewalk but stayed in one spot instead. A push was all he needed to get going. Fritz provided the necessary impetus with a great booming laugh, jump-starting the boy's retreat. As fast as his young feet were capable of carrying him, down the street he ran. Willard watched him go.

Soon, Fritz partially materialized.

"The bone was a bad one, Willy. I lost a hunting dog to poison, so I know the smell. You might not have picked up on it until you'd already chomped on it a few times. I've got to be off, Willard. I think I'm going to teach our young chemist a lesson. Should be fun. I'll see you later."

Willard understood everything Fritz said. He owed the Laird of Dunbar his life, and dogs, if they're anything at all, are loyal and grateful. To show his gratitude, he stood up on his hind feet and did an upper two-paw begging salute. Feeling a ghostly hand pat the top of his head, Willard attempted a lick but found nothing of a corporeal nature to apply his affection to. With Fritz's departure, the lucky dog returned to the inside of the house to find Sonya already dressed and looking for her moped keys.

"Come on, Willy, we've got to go to town. I want to talk with the Sheriff about what we learned last night. Find your sweater. It's actually a bit chilly outside." She picked up the terrier and gave him a kiss on the top of his head. "I love you, Willy. You're my baby."

And that, dear reader, is why Fritz is more heart than horror. He knows what matters to those he loves. No one messes with the Laird of Dunbar, or his family.

Scene Break

Sonya knew where to find Sheriff Walker that morning. She had, on occasion, seen him having his breakfast at Tilly's Diner, the local coffee drinker's hangout for Willow Valley. On any typical day, between the early hours of six o'clock and nine o'clock, a group of older men from various backgrounds would be at Tilly's eating biscuits and gravy and drinking cup after cup of coffee at their favorite table known by most Willow Valleyians as Table Number Three.

What brought them in was the excellent food, but what kept them around were the bottomless cups of caffeine and heated discussions on everything from government news to the threat of recession. These farmers, tradesmen, and business owners loved nothing better than to talk about the graft in Washington, how the weather was different from last year (or not), and the ridiculous cost of everything.

It was into this oasis of good food and congenial company that Sonya arrived. Table Number Three's voices dropped to a low murmur. She waved at Mr. Thomas, the owner of the feed store, who gave a brief nod in acknowledgment and a smile. There were some subtle whispers exchanged and some eyebrows raised among his tablemates. The word was already out about the events that took place last night at Sonya's séance, but this was immediately forgotten when Marsha, the head waitress handed Earl Higginbotham, a longtime member of Table Three, his ticket.

"Marsha? You've got this ticket wrong. I had one cup of coffee this morning. You've charged me for two," Earl pointed out.

"No mistake, Earl. We've raised out prices," Marsha said walking away and leaving Table Three's men looking shocked at this new revelation.

You should have heard the grumbling. Earl, who owned the Chevy car dealership and could well afford the seventy-five cent increase, pronounced he wouldn't be paying extortionist prices for sub-grade coffee anymore. With a bang of his hand on the table, he declared he'd be drinking water from now on.

No one at Table Three offered a comment and, if truth be told, poor Earl realized a bit too late that he'd played the righteous indignation part a bit too strongly. As everyone knew, Tilly, the owner, easily heard everything from her perch on the barstool she sat on while frying food at the grill.

A response to Earl's outburst didn't take long in coming. The Diva of the Diner sashayed out of the kitchen bringing a chilling silence to the dining room. With a loud, ringing firmness, she set her own special coffee mug emblazoned with a picture of her grandson down on the counter bringing the entire dining area to order. Reverberations from the mug's placement continued to hang in the air like the sound of a judge's gavel after it had been struck against a block.

With a stiffness to their posture, the coffee boys each in their own time turned around to see Tilly standing there with a sour, no-nonsense look on her face. She blinked twice as if to bring her quarry into focus better. The waitress staff scuttled either into the back or found something to do, while the mute coffee guzzlers at Table Three made a diligent effort to search for possible hidden messages among the grounds clumped at the bottom of their cups.

"Earl, I think one good turn deserves another, don't you?" Tilly slowly asked in her gravelly voice as she lowered her steady gaze upon him alone.

Earl lifted his head, and it should be said, with great strength of character he managed to utter a response. "Oh, what would that be, Tilly?"

No one moved. The place was deadly quiet. Tussling with Tilly was like taking on a female honey badger. Only masochists, the ignorant, or those suffering from hubris at their own worthiness ever attempted to tangle with Till. Everyone remembered how one time a man from California had come into the cafe and finding his Southern-style hot roast beef sandwich not up to par with the ones they made in California, he had the plate sent back to the kitchen with a high-handed condescending attitude toward Marsha, his waitress.

On that day, too, Till emerged from her kitchen with her iconic Camel cigarette dangling against all odds from the corner of her mouth and approached his table. Putting the returned meal back down in front of the man, she asked slowly what his problem was with his dinner.

"I didn't get what I ordered. This," he pointed to the plate in front of him in a lofty manner, "is not a roast beef sandwich like we eat in California. I won't eat it, and I won't pay for it."

Tilly studied the obviously well-heeled Californian. Taking the half-smoked cigarette from her mouth and never losing eye contact with the obdurate, rude patron, she lowered her hand and stubbed the cigarette out in the steaming brown pool of gravy saying, "Well, that's your problem isn't it? You're confused. This is Missouri, not California."

Utterly flabbergasted, the man stood up to attempt a rebuttal, but that was the second bad move on his part that day. He raised his finger to point it at Tilly's ponderous bosom, but, he, like Napoleon, never saw his Waterloo coming. Till took the perfectly white, damp kitchen towel she always wore around her neck and with excellent aim, she snapped him right in his prodigious paunch, throwing him completely off-guard.

He swore an oath, to be true, but no sooner was it out of his mouth than she had him by the back of his belt loops and was hustling him out the front door of the diner. At nearly six feet tall, he looked utterly ridiculous walking on his tippy toes as a woman two-thirds of his size hustled him from her establishment. He landed, luckily for him, on both feet while she, without a word, slammed the door to the diner in his face.

So, with that previous expulsion in mind, the boys at Table Three were sitting motionless as Tilly responded back to Earl's question.

"I'm thinking about buying a new car, Earl, and I'd like to buy one from you. There's one catch, though. I want it for the same price I would have paid for it five years ago."

Earl's chest thrust out in indignation. "Tilly, I...I...can't do that."

She had him. Her gaze intensified on him, and she directed her voice in such a way that Earl didn't have any trouble knowing it was him she was talking to.

"Why not? For the last ten years, you've sat on your back end every morning in this cafe paying for one cup of coffee and drinking five. If I do the math, at seventy-five cents times four, times three hundred, times ten, you probably owe me somewhere around nine thousand dollars for all that free coffee you've been drinking."

Table Number Three did the mental calculations and realized Tilly was dead on. They waited to see what Earl would say. Clearing his throat, he said humbly, "You never asked us to pay for the extra coffee, Tilly."

Tilly took a drink from her own coffee mug and replied with a shrug, "That's the point, Earl. I am now. The price has gone up. If you don't want to pay seventy-five cents more for a bottomless cup of coffee, fine. Drink water or drink coffee somewhere else."

It was how she said it, like when your mom shames you after you've done something low or greedy. No drama or histrionics are necessary as slowly and solidly, in that perfect way, she waits to see if you've got the chops to assume your guilt and do the right thing. The boys at Table Number Three felt the sting. Sometimes grumping went too far and this was such a time. Tilly turned and went back to her kitchen, the noise of the restaurant returned to its regular din and Sonya spied Sheriff Zeb sitting hunkered over his plate at the end of the bar trying to not be recognized.

Making her way over, she sat down beside him.

"Good morning, Sheriff. How are you?" she asked brightly.

"Mrs. Caruthers, good to see you again." His words and his tone were at odds with one another. "Why do I get the feeling you've got a question or two for me?"

She got right to the point, but recognizing it was a public place, she kept her voice low. "Last night we met the ghost who is haunting The Whispering Pines RV Park. Her name is Poppy Turner. I thought you would like to know Miss Turner is not alive but dead. She may be the owner of the skeleton you've had removed from the swimming pool pit."

Zeb quickly scanned the diner to make sure no one else had heard or was likely to overhear Sonya's comments.

"Mrs. Caruthers," he said throwing a ten-dollar bill down by his half-finished plate and standing up, "would you please come with me outside. Let's find another place to discuss your...um...findings."

124

Sonya rose and followed Zeb out to his police car.

"This morning, Dale Smith called me. He was very excited to inform us about Poppy Turner and…" Zeb hesitated to continue as if he wasn't sure of the ground he was standing on. "It's not typical police procedure to conduct an investigation on this kind of information. You do understand, don't you?"

Zeb was trying to be as considerate as possible, and Sonya recognized this. She nodded her head and said, "Of course, I understand, but it may save you some time. Look, Sheriff, that's not why I'm here. I wanted to know more about Ryan Houseman and the Turner treasure."

"You've been listening to gossip, Mrs. Caruthers," Zeb said with a knowing smile and a shake of his head. "I'd like you not to ask Ryan questions about Poppy and definitely don't tell him you've been talking with his high school sweetheart's ghost. He's not exactly off our radar regarding this investigation and I don't want you…setting things in motion."

It was a habit of Sonya's when she was asked to do something she didn't agree with to pucker her mouth up and over to one side. She considered Zeb's request. "Normally, I'd be happy to comply, Sheriff, but Poppy is an unhappy, lost soul, and she wants to see Ryan. It's my job to help her. Also, she wants her body buried properly and her murderer, in my opinion, should be brought to justice. Isn't there any way you can work with me on this?"

Zeb blinked a number of times more than necessary and took a deep breath before proceeding. Sonya knew this was new territory, and his body language was saying so.

"I tell you what, Mrs. Caruthers, you give me twenty-four hours, and I'll," he held up his index finger much like a teacher who's about to make a point, "give you the go-ahead to talk whatever spiritual, ghost stuff you need to with Ryan Houseman. Okay?"

Sonya wasn't pleased, but she nodded her assent. She decided not to push it about the treasure and Poppy's husband, Ricky Mitchell. Sheriff Walker opened his car door and got in to start the engine. The conversation was at an end. Sonya stepped back up on the curb and waved 'goodbye' as he backed out onto the road.

If she wanted to do some real digging without affronting her local sheriff, it was time to go to Lana's Beauty Shoppe. The girls at Lana's always knew all the romantic entanglements, the real parentage of most children in town, and the true motivations (financial or emotional) of most business deals struck in Willow Valley.

With Zeb gone, Sonya turned to see Willy snoozing comfortably in his basket on the back of the moped. Patting him on his cute head, she sat down on the vehicle's seat and put on her helmet. It was off to Lana's for a nice cup of coffee, a fresh do of her hair, and some gossiping, Willow Valley ladies' style.

Chapter 18

"This place is filthy!" Melanie Mitchell complained as she picked her way gingerly through the debris of the burnt-out shell of the Turner house.

After Sheriff Walker's visit, Ricky wanted to see for himself what the fire might have unearthed with its destruction. If that treasure the old woman had hidden was still out there, he believed it was rightly his.

"Why did you wear those ridiculous shoes, woman? You're not going to be any help dressed like that," Ricky said irritably, as he tried in vain to lift some fallen timbers from over a charred trap door in the floor. "Why would anybody burn this place down, Melanie? It's like it was done for a reason. Everyone knew about the treasure. It might be burned up now for all we know."

Ricky's better half appeared disinterested in soiling her outfit or her hands with the dirty business of treasure hunting on a condemned site. Melanie sat down on what was left of the stone foundation, let out a bored sigh, and turned the exquisite sapphire ring on her left hand.

"What makes you think it's even here? The treasure was probably a lie. The only treasure, Ricky, was the land itself. It's not likely that there was ever a hoard of money stashed somewhere in this old pile anyway. You said yourself Poppy's mother up and left one day. If there was money, she probably took it with her, Ricky."

Not deterred by his wife's laziness or her disinterest in a possible fortune, Ricky continued his search. He'd freed an entire area of what was once the hallway between the living room and the kitchen. The crows squawked and beat their wings in protest to his interfering presence. Some took to the air calling out their warnings, while a few swooped down to land on the ground not far from the entrance to the lovely barn which had been standing since before the Civil War.

"Those birds scare me," Melanie said eyeing the black-winged creatures who kept a reciprocal watch on her. "They're getting too close."

"They are stupid birds, Mel. Tell'em to shoo, and they'll go away."

With two great heaving efforts, Ricky finally lifted an old trap door in what was left of the house's floor. A fine ash mushroomed up on air currents created from the suction of opening the hatchway.

"Hey, I'm going down. Don't wander off, Mel, in case I need you. No one has been in this cellar for years. This might be where she hid it."

As Ricky descended the cellar steps, a great shot rang out, sending the crows into flight with raucous cries. Melanie bolted upright into a standing position wobbling on two precariously tall high heel shoes, as Ricky twisted around to look up into the air at the flying black birds beating their wings over his head.

"What the hell?" he yelled. "Was that a gunshot, Mel?"

But Melanie wasn't answering; she was already running for their rusty, red pickup truck. It wasn't an easy thing to do in three-inch wedge pumps, but she managed a fast toddling gait in the direction of their truck. As for Ricky, he continued to stare at the sky for signs of the bullet that passed by.

Melanie had no sooner reached the truck's door when another ear-splitting gunshot blasted overhead. Ricky practically levitated vertically from his spot on the first step of the cellar stairs. Pitching himself forward, he stood again like a turkey with his head upturned, as he tried to scan the air for the second bullet's trajectory.

"AAAiiieehhh!" Melanie screamed in reaction to this second eruption. Her own body made a jolting move resembling a windmill doing jumping jacks. At the truck, she frantically worked the door handle. "I'm leaving Ricky!" she screeched. "Get over here, you idiot!"

Being a bit on the portly side, Ricky did his best to scramble over the crunchy, charred remains of two-by-fours and metal remains of ductwork. He made it down what was left of the house's front steps and worked his way to the fired-up getaway truck. Melanie gunned the engine.

As the two stayed low in their front seat in an effort not to be shot, the old, red truck roared down the bumpy dirt road occasionally hitting a pothole, causing it and its contents to bounce and pitch haphazardly, but always in a forward motion. If Ricky or Melanie had turned around, they might have caught sight of a woman emerging from the Turner barn, holding a long shotgun in her grasp.

Ma Turner watched as the billowing dust from the dirt road obscured her view of the Mitchells' departure. She broke out with a great hearty laugh.

"Boy, I wish they'd come back so I could do that all over again. What a treat! I've been wanting to run that worthless piece of human waste off my property for years."

She fired another shot off into the sky.

"Yippee!" she called out with joy. "Ricky Mitchell, I should have planted two of these shells in your back end, but I'm a peace-loving woman, so better to see you run like a worried ninny than feel the guilt of wasting two good shotgun shells on the likes of you. I'll see you rot in jail."

With a happy smile and a gleeful tune, Ma Turner, Poppy's mother, tucked her gun under her arm and went back into the barn. She was back from Australia where she'd spent the last three years living with her daughter, Rose. As for Ricky and Melanie, they wouldn't be skulking around the place again anytime soon. A living Turner woman was back in residence and she wanted justice.

Scene Break

After dropping Willard off at La Pooch Salon for his monthly freshening, Sonya hurried over to Lana's to have some work done on herself as well. As any woman will tell you, the local beauty shop is a delightfully enjoyable place. There are lots of refreshing smells, uplifting treatments to make you feel good, and tasty news, whether it's found in the plethora of magazines or shared by the stylists themselves. There is something comforting about being surrounded by the chatty, camaraderie of the small town beauty shop.

"Why, hello, Sonya," Lana called warmly from the back of the shop. "Your timing is great. I just finished Mrs. McGillicuddy's perm. Have a seat, and I'll be right with you."

She pointed to her station's chair, which, in and of itself, was a true work of art. Lana's theme for her shop was rhinestone cowgirl meets pink princess, which meant every station's chair was done up in shiny leather the color of strawberry Shasta cola and so much bling a girl had to feel special just sitting down in it.

Sonya gave a friendly wave to Lindi, Jaxon, and Sabrianna, the stylists, as she walked past. They each smiled, but it was Jaxon who stopped his razoring a pixie cut in mid-whack to say, "Mrs. Caruthers, it's all over town this morning that you had a séance in your parlor and you raised the dead!"

All the rest of the beauty shop crowd made noises of awe and delight. Sabrianna, who was wrapping a lady's hair with tin foil and applying color, shivered dramatically and exclaimed, "Please, Mrs. Caruthers, invite me next time. I've got to get in touch with my Aunt Belle. She's the only person who knows if my brother, Lou, is my daddy's real son."

Sonya laughed. "Sabrianna, I'm not touching that one with a ten-foot pole. Sounds like Aunt Belle might not be happy with you poking your nose into that kind of family trouble. She might blow up a storm in my house to teach you a lesson and, believe me, it has happened before."

Again, lots of thrilled oohs and aahhs from the clientele. Sabrianna laughed and continued her work. As everyone got back to their regular conversations, Popcorn, Lana's grandchild poodle about the size of a football came over to Sonya wagging her tail in greeting.

Sonya walked over to Lana's pink bedazzled client chair. "I see you're doing better, Popcorn," she said picking up the pint-sized dog and holding it in her lap. "You shouldn't eat from the trash can, Popcorn. Willard could tell you stories about the things Dr. Landon, the vet, has X-rayed in his stomach."

Popcorn, content with her ears being scratched, curled up in a fluffy ball on Sonya's lap.

"That dog costs me more than some of my kids did," Lana said with a sigh, putting a bright purple cape around Sonya's neck. "I've told Zebadiah I'm not going to constantly dog sit while he's at work every day."

She patted the sleeping dog on Sonya's lap.

"Lana?" Sonya asked.

"Yes."

"Is there any chance you are Sheriff Walker's mother?"

"I claim him. He's mine." Lana fluffed Sonya's hair a bit and gave her a long, penetrating assessment. "Do you want to add some fun highlights? I think a strip of lavender would be pretty."

"Would it have to be dark?" Sonya asked giving the idea some consideration.

"Just a hint of color. What do you think?"

"If you promise it will be light, I think it would be pretty."

Lana was excited and rambled off to the back area to mix the color. She continued to talk as she worked.

"Zeb's my firstborn and still not married." She pointed to the cup-sized poodle in Sonya's lap. "He's got a child, but it runs on all fours. You'd think from looking at him, he'd have a wife, but keeps telling me he hasn't met the right one yet. Why do you ask?"

"Last night, at the spiritual therapy session…" Sonya noticed Lana's look of confusion through the mirror. "Okay, the séance."

Lana nodded at the revision, so Sonya restarted her line of thought.

"Anyway, the point is that the spirit we contacted talked about the Turner Treasure. Do you know anything about that?"

Picking Popcorn up off Sonya's lap and putting her in the doggy bed near the warm clothes dryer, Lana said, "Didn't want Zeb's dog to have purple dots on her. Sometimes this hair dye can get away from me. Yes, everyone knows about the infamous treasure. This morning, Dale Smith, Marnie's handyman and our town crier, let it be known your spirit last night was Poppy Turner." Lana shook her head at the tragedy of it all. "It's being whispered, Sonya, that Poppy was killed for that treasure and people are pointing fingers at Ricky, her husband."

Sonya pursed her lips in consternation. The last thing

she wanted was someone to be blamed for something they might not have done.

"Lana, if you would, let it be known that Poppy, herself, didn't believe it was Ricky. I don't want gossip to get in the way of the sheriff's investigation."

"Oh, girl, don't play a player," Lana teased, "that's why you're here; for the gossip."

Both women chuckled conspiratorially. "Okay, okay, you're right, but tell me what you know about the treasure. I think it may have something to do with Poppy's story."

"When Kathy Berkowitz and Ryan Houseman were youngsters in high school, they dated each other. Everyone thought they'd be married, but things never go smoothly where love is concerned. Poppy Turner was a beautiful girl, and one day she took a liking to Ryan. It was Mother Nature mixing things up and poor Kathy lost out. To be honest, people whispered unkind things about Poppy and blamed her. No one ever considered it was Ryan who walked away from Kathy. People always want to blame a woman. Never fails."

"It was a sad situation for all three in some way, wasn't it?" Sonya said more than asked. "How did Kathy handle it?"

"She went away to a college in Texas and no one saw her for a few years. She got married. Very successful but I heard she divorced her husband and moved back to a town close by. As for Ryan and Poppy, they broke up a year after Kathy left. Got into a fight over something, and to make Ryan jealous, Poppy married Ricky Mitchell a year later. They were together for at least six or seven years. Poppy was pretty, but simple. Marrying Ricky was a colossal mistake."

"What happened to Ryan?" Sonya asked.

"He's taken over his family's tractor supply business and never married. Most people think he's waiting for Poppy to come back to him. Ryan nearly killed Ricky one day down in front of Puggly's Grocery Store. He demanded to know where Poppy was, and Ricky called her a whore and claimed she ran off with some man from a neighboring town. It was my Zeb, who pulled Ryan off Ricky. Good thing he did, because Ryan would have killed Ricky. They've kept to the opposite side of the road ever since."

"Did Ricky remarry or begin to live lavishly?"

Lana laughed out loud. "Come on, I need to rinse you."

As she made Sonya comfortable in the shampoo bowl, she continued her story. "Ricky has since remarried a woman named Melanie. Some say they were stepping out long before Poppy ran off with her new lover from Springville. Today, they run a fertilizer farm on the other side of town and by no means do they live an extravagant lifestyle. If the treasure was ever found, it wasn't by those two."

"What exactly do people think the treasure was, and who is supposed to have hidden it?"

"The Turner's were actually wealthy farmers. All that land around the old house, down next to The Whispering Pines RV Park and right up to Willow Valley itself, was Turner property. They'd been here since before the Civil War, and Poppy Turner and her sister, Rose, were heiresses in every sense of the word." Lana's voice lowered to a whisper. "Some estimate those girls were worth over ten million dollars."

Sonya sat dumbfounded, seated once again in the pink rhinestone chair.

"That's a reason to kill, if ever I heard one," she said softly.

"Honey, that's why I know it wasn't Ricky and Melanie. They'd have been gone in three shakes of a bear's tail if they'd gotten hold of the money."

Nodding in agreement, Sonya sat quietly for a while until Lana began snipping with her scissors at the ends of her hair.

"So the real value was in the land, but it must have been sold off over time. No one lives at the Turner place anymore, do they?"

"No. It's been abandoned since Poppy left or died, and Ricky moved in with Melanie. Rose and the girl's mother, Nellie Turner, were disgusted by Poppy marrying Ricky and Nellie never made any bones about it. Nellie stayed on for a long time and finally left. Supposedly, it was because they'd married and she didn't want Ricky to ever get his hands on Poppy's money."

"Where did she go?" Sonya asked.

"Nellie left to go live in Australia with Rose, who married some boy she met on a trip to Europe and that was the last anyone ever saw of her. From what I've heard, Poppy and Ricky fought all the time about money. Nellie always sent them money to live on, but it was never enough some people say for Ricky. He smelled more and wanted to get his hands on it."

Lana was drying Sonya's hair. The lavender highlight came down next to her face. It was exactly the softness in hue that Lana had promised it would be.

"I love the color, Lana. You were right to suggest it. Thank you," Sonya said with a bright smile of gratitude.

"Darling, it makes me happy to see my customers leave feeling good. Glad to do it."

Sonya paid Lana, along with an extra-hefty tip for the information, and went outside to get on her moped. Wishing it wasn't necessary to put on her helmet after having her hair done, she looked in the round side mirror and admired her new do. With a sigh, she strapped the helmet on and puttered down the pretty, tree-lined road to go rescue Willard from La Pooch Salon. It had been an enlightening morning, and it was time to consider another conversation with Poppy.

Chapter 19

The afternoon was warm and sunny. A soft, muggy breeze hinted at the summer weather to be expected for southern Missouri. Mr. Pepper and Mr. Simpson were lounging in two comfortable hammocks hung on stands under giant-sized pine trees whose green boughs moved intermittently in the soft wind.

As the two men snored in and out on opposite beats, Lewis and Clark came loping into this tranquil scene.

"I thought that was the smell of hot dogs, Lewis. They've left 'em lying on the table so they must be done eating. What do ya think?" Clark asked hopefully, his nose sniffing at the edge of the table where three plump hot dogs rested on a paper plate.

"Yeah, let's take care of those for the two humans. It would be a shame to see them left there for much longer. Besides, those crows who hang around here will grab them if we don't," Lewis added. He put his two front paws up on the table and shook it making the hot dogs roll off onto the ground. Clark was quick to snatch two, leaving the other one for his brother.

Down near the pavilion, Dale was working. The lawnmower he was using made a humming sound that added to the peaceful ambiance of the park that afternoon.

With the hot dogs eaten, Lewis and Clark decided to lie in the shade under Mr. Pepper's hammock. Soon, they, too, were asleep. A creaking from above made Lewis drowsily open the one eye not mashed against the grass. He heard a soft female voice humming, much the same way Marnie would do when she was folding clothes or making dinner. From Lewis' vantage point, it looked like two people were lying in Mr. Pepper's hammock. *"Odd that,"* Lewis thought to himself.

Lulled by the music, he let his one eye droop shut again and he drifted back to his favorite doggy paradise, a place filled with donuts, bacon, and slow squirrels.

AAAhrrrruuushhh! A blast of unnatural wind and what sounded like two angry squirrels nattering and attacking each other brought Mr. Pepper, Mr. Simpson, and Lewis and Clark abruptly out of their naps.

Whatever it was causing the tempest, couldn't be seen, but the air around the camp was swirling and things were being tossed around in every direction. Lewis and Clark both rose up at the same time, upending Mr. Pepper from his hammock, while screeching female sounds and hostile charges were being made across the two men's hammocks.

The two beagles, knowing when it was a good time to make their exit, flew from the disaster zone at top speed toward the safety of home. Noah Simpson managed to get out of his swinging fabric bed and made a dash for his own camper, but halfway to the door, he hesitated. Maybe being locked inside again with another unnatural entity wasn't a good idea, so, instead, he ran for Marnie's place.

"Stop it! Stop it!" Mr. Pepper yelled while lying on the

ground. "I'm tired of being tossed about, and I'm tired of all this hullabaloo. Just stop it!"

The storm ceased around him.

"Eloise, if that's you, I'm leaving on Sunday after the dance. I promise to get back to Canton and take care of the Jeff situation for Casey. As for whoever it is you're having a fuss with, she needs to get on home, too. Both of you settle down, go your separate ways, and leave me be!"

Mr. Pepper finished up with an irritated 'harrumph' and stomped inside his camper, but before he shut his door, he leaned back outside a bit and said, "And don't either one of you come inside. Stay out!" He slammed the door.

It was clear he'd had enough of ghostly female trouble. As for Eloise, she heard by his tone, he intended to head home in a few days and that was all she wanted from him anyway. Poppy hovered over her pit, not sure what to do with herself.

"Don't you have anywhere to go other than that hole in the ground?" Eloise asked Poppy in an irritated voice.

"I had a home, but it burned down. That's why I've been coming around here," Poppy sobbed.

"Oh, for goodness sakes! You've got to pull yourself together. You may be dead, but you're not done. Why are you hanging around anyway? I'm trying to see to some family problems with my daughter and grandchildren, so what's your story?" Eloise said in a tough maternal tone.

"Well, I think someone killed me and I wasn't buried," she pointed to the pit, "in a decent way. I feel like I need to say goodbye to the people I loved."

Eloise did understand. Ghosts who had bad ends tended to struggle with the afterlife sometimes.

"I see. It makes sense now. Well, I don't have time for this, but I guess I kind of owe you one for inadvertently helping me to light a fire under Saul's butt to go home to Casey."

Eloise studied Poppy for a short second. "I'll go with you to your old home and see what can't be done to make you more comfortable. As for the goodbyes and the burial, that's on you."

Poppy nodded. "I think those are being taken care of by a woman. I would like to go home, though."

The two ghosts wandered off through the woods in the direction of the Turner House and farm. It wasn't long before they reached the place. A campfire was smoking with the homey smell of meat being grilled.

"There's someone here," Poppy said surprised.

"It's a woman. A pitiful dresser, though," Eloise added.

"Hey! That's my mama!" Poppy exclaimed.

"Don't go running up at her, you ninny. It'll scare her. Trust me; I've scared the daylights out of my daughter. Go slow and do something gentle that lets you be close to her but not give her a heart attack."

As Poppy walked away in the direction of her mother who was scratching around trying to tidy up her burnt-out shell of a home, Eloise disappeared. Poppy would be fine. Everyone, at some point, had to get used to being dead around the living. It was a normal rite of passage. Life goes on, just in different ways.

Chapter 20

Putting the finishing touches on his spiky, tough-cop hairdo, Deputy Kirchner gave himself a critical look in the mirror. He'd taken special care today to look his best. His shoes were buffed to a beautiful black shine, and he was wearing his uniform he kept for special occasions, which he always had laundered at the dry cleaners.

"Maybe I've overdone it. I don't want to look like I'm trying too hard to impress her," he said to himself, feeling worried. Remembering Dr. Dempster, Tommy decided it was better to put his best foot forward. If Dempster was around, he'd be watching to see how Tommy handled himself.

"Okay," he said straightening himself up to his full five-foot-eleven height. "Let's go see Laney." At the sound of her name, his stomach dropped a few inches. This visceral reaction was a clear indication of his true feelings.

Before Tommy headed to Dr. Dempster's office, he needed to stop off at the police station to retrieve the forensic file on the skeleton. His drive to work was an incredibly short five minutes.

For the last five years, Tommy had been living in an apartment over Mrs. Maglioni's restaurant. It suited his bachelor needs. Plus, from the time he woke up to the time he walked into work, it was a thirty-minute turnaround. Today, though, he'd been primping for over an hour.

"Morning, Tommy," Zeb said, watching his starched and pressed glamor-deputy walk through the reception area. "You going to a funeral today?" he teased, knowing full well, Tommy was off to see Laney at Dr. Dempster's office about the dental records.

A bit piqued at Zeb's teasing, Tommy gruffly replied, "Nope, you know I'm going to Dr. Dempster's this morning. Want to look my best."

Men give no quarter usually in the area of torture teasing their friends. So, Zeb continued his playful attempts at annoying his favorite deputy.

"Well, I think I need you to run an errand today up to Pineville instead of going to see the tempting Laney."

Zeb lifted his eyes from the papers on his desk in time to see Tommy's crestfallen expression at the horror of having to go to Pineville instead of Dr. D's. It was too much fun, and the sheriff gave up trying to hold in his laughter.

"Boy! You look like my dog, Popcorn, did when I took away the chicken bone she got a hold of and was chewing on last night. I'm messing with you, deputy. Get on over and see Laney. Don't waste all morning over there, though. We do need to drive up to Pineville today. I've got a new recruit I need you to help train."

Zeb put two fingers to his mouth and whistled loudly. In came the dog he'd rescued from Ricky and Melanie's the

143

day before. It had been bathed, treated for fleas, and looked, at least, fifty percent better.

"Here's your police dog you've been wanting," Zeb said, his tone as excited as a parent who is giving the best Christmas present ever to his kid. "Took her to the vet yesterday and they said she's a mix between a German Shepherd and a Labrador. Should make a great dog to train. Dr. Landon said she's not quite two years old. Her former situation was a bad one, so you'll need to be gentle. We're going to Pineville to sign you both up for the classes."

If Tommy hadn't restrained himself, he would have crossed the short distance between him and the sheriff to give the former a massive hug. Having never had a dog before and wanting one for so long, the joy of it nearly made him tear up. He'd kept himself from having one simply because of his job. It would be unfair to any dog not to spend time with it.

He went over and offered his mentor a handshake. Upon reflection (and because no one else was around), he went ahead and gave Zeb a hug.

"Thank you, sir. I won't let you down. I'd like to name her Sheba," he said.

"I know you won't let me down. That's a good name for her. Heck, those boys in Pineville, after looking at you today, will think I'm running a top-notch program down here."

Zeb watched the young man rough-up the dog's fur, which sat slavishly at his new human's feet.

"Don't spoil her too much, and she needs to live with

you. If Mama Maglioni won't let you have her in your apartment, you're going to have to find other arrangements. Got it?"

Tommy's smile stretched from one ear to the other, "Not a problem. Mrs. Maglioni loves me because she thinks no one will rob her if I'm living up above the restaurant. With this dog's hearing and fierce barking, she's gonna feel that much safer."

"Okay, better be going, deputy. Leave the dog here until you're done at Dr. Dempster's. She can help me do paperwork."

Tommy grabbed his computer and the forensic files and headed out to his car after petting the dog one last time. As he settled himself in the car seat and put on his safety belt, his mind snapped back to his conversation with Mrs. Caruthers on her front porch the day before.

"She couldn't have known, could she...about the dog?" he said under his breath. "It's a female and Zeb said it came from a difficult situation."

Tommy shook his head, but a smile creased the corners of his mouth. If Mrs. Caruthers was right, maybe he had a shot with Laney, too. He backed the police vehicle out of the parking spot, took one last look in his rearview mirror to see Sheba peeking out at him through the station's windows watching him pull away.

Scene Break

Sonya, home from her fact-finding mission, watched

145

Willard roll around in her back garden determined to remove the soap smell from the bath they gave him at La Pooch Salon. The pretty bow was hanging loosely to the side of his head. She shook her head and went inside.

It had been a busy day and she wanted to take off her shoes, make a cup of coffee, and relax. Halfway to the fruition of her dream, Fritz blew in with a fury. He made the copper pots hanging over her range rattle and clank together inharmoniously.

"I'm glad you're finally home, Sonya. I'm not living under this roof a minute longer with that clingy, whiny female from the dirt pit. She won't leave me alone and I tossed her out of the house."

Fritz called Sonya by her given name instead of Sunny only when he was truly upset.

"Fritz!" Sonya exclaimed. "Where did she go?"

"Back to her hole, no doubt. I could care less. It was like wrenching myself free from an eight-legged Caoineag."

"A what?" Sonya asked.

"A Caoineag. It's a whining Scottish banshee who brings gloom and death," Fritz said with an overstated bored irritation.

"Oh for Pete's sake, Fritz, it hasn't been that difficult. Poppy can't kill you; you're already dead. Let's go find her and bring her back. She needs to be at peace, or you know how this can go."

Half materialized, Fritz sat on top of the kitchen cabinets looking gloomy for a minute, not responding to

Sonya's call for action. She saw by his face, he wasn't going to help her.

"What is it, Fritz? Did something happen that's upset you?"

He hemmed and hawed while fiddling with the saltshaker that sat on the stovetop. Finally, he said, "I can see something you can't and it…" he shook his head like he was trying to chase the image from his mind.

"What? What can't I see?" Sonya demanded.

Fritz compressed his lips together in a gesture of disgust.

"It's always like this with the murdered ones, Sonya," he said in a softer voice. "For some reason, the living can't see the damage done to them like we can. They live a half-life and they're haunted. To make it right, they need to ascend to God. While she was in the ground, she wasn't likely to shift, but unless she finds someone to cling to soon, she may go bad. It's disturbing for the rest of us. They pull on our energy. I can't have her so close."

Sonya understood Fritz's concern. Spirits like Poppy needed immediate action to save them. They were incredibly difficult to help because they could lose all sense of time, connectedness to their real lives, and for some, they became too dark to save. Black energy holes that lost all semblance of their souls.

For some reason, murder victims, if they didn't take their first opportunity to ascend, might wander for eons as perpetual victims or begin to descend into a spiritual madness. Other ghosts might try to help, but it was like trying to communicate with an infant. Sonya realized time was short for Poppy. She'd been buried and the ground had kept her safe, perhaps, but the minute she was unearthed and her home removed, time started ticking for her.

"Okay, Fritz. I know you can't have her too close, but I need you to tell me where you think she is. If I'm going to help her, I need you to find her."

"I'll do it for you, love, but afterwards. I'm off to see my kin for a while. My wife has invited me for a walk along Loch Lomond. I'll be taking the low road, for sure, but as for her, she's already there and it's not for me to keep her waiting. You understand don't you, Sunny?"

"Of course, and it's the right thing to do, Fritz. All good Scotsmen go home."

Fritz sat quietly with no disturbance from either Sonya or Willard, who trotted in carrying in his mouth one of the legs from his favorite rubber chicken. The soft patter of rain tapped on the kitchen windowsill, breaking the silence of the room.

"She's gone home, Sunny, not the dirt hole where they buried her, but her house. Better get cracking on finding her lover, he's the one she needs to say goodbye to. She won't budge until that's been done. Better get her buried, too. When I get back, I promise to help round up her killer. He's got a mark. They always do."

Fritz sang a familiar tune as he dematerialized and left on his journey home. Sonya could hear it as if it came from somewhere far away. It was one we all know.

By yon bonnie banks and by yon bonnie braes,
Where the sun shines bright on Loch Lomond,
Where me and my true love were ever wont to go,
On the bonnie, bonnie banks o' Loch Lomond.

Chorus:
O ye'll take the high road, and I'll take the low road,
And I'll be in Scotland afore ye,
But me and my true love are meant to meet again,
On the bonnie, bonnie banks o' Loch Lomond.

The wee birdies sing and the wildflowers spring,
And in sunshine the waters are sleeping.
But the broken heart it can, never second spring again,
Though the woeful may cease from their grieving.

Sonya listened as the tune faded, becoming indistinct and more like the wind than a song. The last stanza was the most heartbreaking, and she thought about how appropriate the verses were for poor Poppy and her lover, Ryan. They would never be together again on this plane. The best way to give them both peace was to help bring their grieving to an end. Sonya knew what she had to do, and it meant getting sideways with Sheriff Walker. There was no time to wait.

Chapter 21

In May, Missouri can be a delightful place. Cool mornings, followed by warm days, provide the perfect weather for flowering trees like redbuds and crabapples to grow colorful blooms of pink, purple, and white. It was a heady time when all living things took an opportunity to show off their spring finery.

They say 'in spring a young man's fancy turns to thoughts of love' and this was definitely true of Tommy Kirchner. Since talking with Laney Bodwell on the phone, the deputy had been in a bit of a dither, thinking about Dr. Dempster's office manager.

He'd found it difficult to keep his mind on his work. What if she was dating someone? This last thought he always tried to banish from his mind with a quick shake of his head. Parking the car in front of Dr. D.'s office, Tommy was careful not to look at himself in the rearview mirror. He didn't want to look like he was primping. Instead, he used his cell phone's reverse camera. It looked all good.

"If she is dating someone, fine," he told himself, realizing he'd spoken out loud and immediately scanning the parking lot to make sure no one saw a Willow Valley officer of the law talking to himself.

"Get it together, man," he chastised himself mentally.

Opening the car door and reminding himself one more time to act professionally, Tommy grabbed the laptop and the forensic file and shut the door. This time, when he saw the wobbling hair bun shoved through with a pencil, he was ready.

"Percy?"

"That's my name," came a chirpy reply and a head popped up as well. "Ah! Deputy Kirchner, I'll bet you're here to have your teeth cleaned."

Percy gave Tommy a brilliantly toothy grin while tilting his head to one side in a gesture of assessment. The smile was excited yet disconcerting at the same time. With a fluidity of movements, Percy was up and hustling Tommy to the back.

"Wait," the deputy tried to slow Percy's train down, "I'm not having my teeth cleaned for another four months, I think. Anyway...that's not why I'm here."

The thin, lanky man-bun-wearing receptionist ignored Tommy's protests and pointed to the dentist's chair as he rattled around in the cabinets.

"Honey, I'm just doing my job. I was told Laney would be doing a cleaning on you this afternoon." He turned to face Tommy and in a low whisper with eyebrows highly elevated for effect, "Dr. D's idea. It's a little test, if you know what I mean."

Percy leaned back with one hand resting on his hip and lowered one eyebrow while leaving the other arched and his mouth pursed.

"Decisions, decisions, deputy. Personally, I'd get in the chair and pray she didn't find anything disgusting in there." Percy pointed with his thumb in the direction of the hallway and whispered, "That man is tricky. It's his way or the highway, guarantee you that."

Tommy assumed the position in the chair and let Percy wrap a bib around his neck. This time the poster was of a dancing white tooth holding a toothbrush and wearing a dress. Trying not to feel or look ridiculous, Tommy waited for Laney to come in.

It was her laughter he heard first. An involuntary smile broke across his face at the sound of it. Full of melody and mirthful rolling notes, the laugh was a contagious one, making those who heard it, or maybe shared in it, feel a sense of joy. While they'd been in school, everyone had loved and courted Laney's laugh.

"Tommy!" she exclaimed coming around in front of him. She reached down and gave him a warm hug. "It's so good to see you. I know we live in the same town, but I truly haven't seen you since graduation. Looks like you've been busy." Smiling, she reached down and lightly touched the badge above his left chest pocket.

He'd been so taken by her entrance and her devastating beauty, that, for a moment, he didn't answer her. If it was possible for a woman to radiate sweetness, Laney did. A fierce truth suddenly struck him. He loved her and he always had. How could a man ever treat her cruelly or indifferently? Her ex-husband must have been a soulless brute.

She blinked waiting for his response.

"I've been busy," was all he was able to say in return.

Laney smiled softly. She fingered the kiddy bib lying across his chest. "Yes, I can see that and it looks good on you."

"The bib?"

"No, the uniform under it."

He couldn't think of anything to say back. His mind reeled for a minute.

"Are you really going to clean my teeth?" he asked with a half chuckle.

"Yep, I am."

She'd already sat down behind him and lowered him into position. Reaching up, she flicked on the overhead light and said, "Open up and let's see what Dr. Dempster was talking about when he said your mother would be mad as a hornet."

"Tammbee..." he said, trying to say her name, but her metal tools were already tapping around inside his mouth.

"Hmmm, yes, let's get you fixed up, and afterwards, we can take a look at those forensic files."

Twenty minutes later, after his teeth were cleaned and they'd laughed about the silly antics of their teenage years, Tommy followed Laney back to her office where all the dental records were kept.

"I've been going through the files to narrow down women who would have been customers in the age group you gave Dr. D. yesterday," Laney said, reaching down below her desk and pulling up a stack of about five manila folders.

"The woman would have been approximately thirty years of age at death." Tommy pulled the forensic report out and showed Laney the details of the skeleton's upper and lower jaw. Multiple radiographs, or X-rays, showed different angles of the upper and lower rows of teeth.

"Do you see this?" she said pointing to one of the postmortem X-rays of the upper jawbone. "It shows that this person had a crown on her first upper right molar. Also, down on the lower jaw on this X-ray, you see that the back two molars on the lower left have filings. All we need to do is go through our list of possibilities to make the match."

"Who do you have fitting the time frame?" Tommy asked.

"Age was my first criteria. The women had to be between twenty-five and thirty years of age one to two years ago. That actually gave me twenty-seven women initially. Then I removed those women I was certain were alive, deceased or had moved."

"How did you account for the ones who'd moved?" Tommy asked.

"Once I removed the living and the deceased, I telephoned the others. There were   four left to find. I was able to speak with three of the women who had moved while one had died in a car accident and was buried. Her family members attended her funeral."

"Are you certain? Were you able to find a death certificate?"

"Oh yes, and once those four were removed from the pile, that left these three. I couldn't find information on them. They are Rose Turner, Poppy Turner, and Autumn Campbell."

"Rose Turner is supposed to be living in Australia. I'll check on her, but what about Autumn Campbell? Any ideas on her?" Tommy asked.

"Autumn is in the Army and it's like pulling teeth to get confirmation from the United States military. That's going to take some time. Her family moved years ago. I think Autumn's case, Tommy, is in your wheelhouse of expertise. The Army will want official documentation. But, look at this. I don't think you need to worry much about Autumn, because if we compare the radiographs of Poppy Turner at twenty-five and the radiographs from your forensic report, you'll see they are an exact match!"

They studied the four sets of radiographs on the light board and without a doubt, there was the crown on the first upper right molar and the two fillings on the bottom back left two molars.

"If that isn't enough proof, this X-ray shows something particular to Poppy. The front two teeth are slightly separated like the ones in Poppy's premortem X-rays. If you asked some people who knew her, and maybe Dr. D. will remember, they might know if she did have a gap between her two front teeth."

Tommy gave Laney an admiring grin. "You would make an incredible detective. You've done some great work here."

"It's been fun, actually. I liked narrowing down the field of possibilities. I've always wanted to go back to school."

Tommy jumped on her idea with enthusiasm. "You should. Maybe forensic dentistry. It would be tough, but you were always a good student in school. It shouldn't be too hard for someone like you."

Laney looked at him with an odd expression on her face.

"What is it? Did I say something wrong?" he asked concerned he'd stuck his foot in his mouth accidentally.

"You thought I was smart in school?" she asked with a perplexed look.

He stared at her for a second, not sure where the conversation was going, but he nodded in the affirmative and answered, "Yeah, Laney, you always made good grades, and look at you now, running this entire office. You've definitely got the intellectual and organizational chops to handle college."

Laney kept looking through the files, her mood appearing distracted.

"Tommy," she said, looking at him with eyes that had known mistrust and deep hurt, "do you mean what you said? Dr. D. is always telling me I should go back to school, but he's like a dad to me, so I thought he was just being sweet."

"Why have you forgotten about how well you did in school, Laney?"

It took a few moments, but when she did speak, it was with uncertainty.

"My husband, Jacob, was…well he did a number on my confidence. We were married a few years, but it took three of those years to finally get the courage to leave him."

She shivered.

"Let's not talk about it anymore," Laney said with a smile. "It's been so nice seeing you and remembering old times."

Tommy knew the kind of man Jacob was. One who liked to demoralize women and make them feel worthless because he hated himself so much. Working domestic violence cases, at least one a month, had taught Tommy that brutes like Jacob were a dime a dozen.

"Hey," he said softly and waited for her to look up into his eyes. "You can do anything you put your mind to, Laney Bodwell, *anything*. As for Jacob, I feel sorry for him."

She smiled and asked, "Why do you feel sorry for that jerk?"

Tommy probably blushed when he answered, but it would prove to be the second best four words he would ever utter in his life.

"Because he lost you."

Sonya never missed the mark on the loves and losses in the lives of the humans she knew. That day, for some reason, the universe wanted Tommy Kirchner to fall in love, get a new dog and give both of those souls a chance at a better future. Some days are good that way.

Chapter 22

The rainstorm was a gentle summer affair with no strong gusts or sharp rips of lightning to split the nighttime sky. Evening had come and occasionally, a soft rumbling rolled across the valley, giving everyone who heard it a tug on their deepest senses of what it meant to be a creature that lived on this mysterious, beautiful planet.

Sonya donned her canary yellow raincoat and red rubber boots. Grabbing both an umbrella and some pepper spray, she headed for the garage to get her green 1959 Morris Minor. Not exactly the most trustworthy machine, it would do the trick when wet weather threatened.

Willard was going as well, but he had to stay in the car. His bath was still fresh and Sonya hoped he'd stay mud-free for at least forty-eight hours.

"It's just you and me, Willy. Fritz is trying to work things out with his wife, so we don't have backup. We're off to go see Ryan Houseman about Poppy. She needs to see him, even though it might put me in some trouble with the sheriff."

Willard was delighted by this proposal because, like most dogs, he loved going somewhere in the car. Sonya had picked up the keys with the red dangling toy bus indicating her solid intent that they were traveling by enclosed vehicle. This also meant they would stop and get ice cream at the Dairyette at some point in the trip. Willard practically pranced out to the car.

It was a short trip to Ryan Houseman's tractor dealership. The streetlights of Willow Valley were alight and made a soft, yellow glare through the Morris' rain-soaked windshield. Not having the best pair of windshield wipers made the going slow, but at last, she pulled the car into Houseman's Tractor, Inc. The exterior lights were not on, causing Sonya to fear everyone had left for the evening, but on closer inspection, she saw a large pickup truck parked alongside the building giving her a ray of hope.

As she stopped her car, Willard whined softly.

"None of that, Willy. After we've finished with our job tonight, we can get our ice cream treat."

Something down inside of Sonya wavered as she turned off the motor. Ryan Houseman didn't know her at all. He would probably think she was a nutty lady if she went in there and told him a story about séances and affectionate ghosts who had lost their way. It might get dicey, for sure.

Taking herself in hand, Sonya got out of the car. It wouldn't hurt to try. Sticking her neck out had landed her in trouble before. But, Poppy needed help. If Houseman told her to get lost, so be it, she'd find another way.

"Be good, Willard," she said to his intelligent, upturned face. He settled back down on his blanket in a position that told her he understood. With the door shut and the umbrella opened, Sonya went up to the main entrance. Best to be direct, she thought.

Upon stepping up to the massive glass windows that flanked one entire side of the showroom, Sonya saw a long, tall reception desk and behind it, barely visible from the top, was a man's head. The head moved, occasionally, as if in a reading motion or working on a computer. As Sonya got closer, a motion detector must have picked up her movements turning on a bright light directly above the entrance doors.

Like it or not, she'd been seen. There was no going back. A nice-looking man in his early thirties stood up from the desk with a questioning expression.

Sonya smiled confidently and raised her hand in a gesture of greeting. The man waved awkwardly and returned a weak smile. He moved hesitantly from behind the reception desk and walked through the showroom toward her. As he reached the glass doors where she stood, he scanned the parking lot.

Without unlocking the door, he called through the glass, "How may I help you?"

Sonya took a deep breath and said, "Mr. Houseman?"

The man's forehead furrowed and his eyes squinted, but he answered, "Yes."

"Ryan Houseman?" Sonya said, realizing she hadn't made sure he didn't have a brother or another Houseman family member who might work here as well.

"I'm Ryan Houseman. Is there something I can help you with?"

He continued to stare at her uncertainly.

Sonya spoke loudly. "My name is Sonya Caruthers

and…well…I need to talk with you about Poppy Turner."

She saw that her last two words had stunned him. He'd had his hand on the door, but at her mentioning of Poppy's name, he drew back like the glass was hot to the touch and shook his head.

"Don't come around here, ma'am, saying that name unless you're here to tell me she's alive."

Sonya's heart dropped into her stomach. She saw the pain in his eyes. To make this action of hers right, she had to keep pushing forward.

"Ryan, I'm sorry, but I need to talk with you. If you won't open the door, please come to my home where we can discuss what's happened to Poppy. I live at 3 Pickwick Street."

Taking one of her cards from her coat pocket, she slid it through the gap between the two doors. He took the card and looked at it. Reaching up, he flipped the lock and opened the door.

"Please come in, Mrs. Caruthers. I guess whatever it is you have to say, can't hurt. Come on over to my desk, and have a seat."

She followed him back to where he'd been before and they sat down across from each other. He gave her an uncertain smile as if to say, "Well?" Sonya jumped in with her best approach.

"Ryan, the other day you may have heard that a body was found in a half-dug pit at The Whispering Pines RV Park. On that same day, one of the residents there was awakened by an unusual experience. His name was Mr.

Saul Pepper and, though you may find this hard to believe, it was a spirit of a woman who did the waking."

No movement from Ryan, but Sonya knew from his expression, he regretted letting her in the door. She hurried on with her tale.

"I know you're thinking that I'm a loony, but this spirit introduced herself on the next day as Poppy."

Ryan sat motionless. After a few seconds, he ran his hands through his hair. Sonya continued, "I believe it was Poppy Turner, and she has asked to see you."

Sonya waited. Ryan studied her with narrowed eyes for a long moment as if he smelled something bad. His nostrils flared, and he shook his head slowly.

"This is crazy. Lady, I don't know whether to ask you to leave or call the hospital to have them come pick you up. As for using Poppy Turner's name to get in here tonight, you better hope this hasn't been a ploy by you or someone else to break in here."

He reached down under his desk and pulled out a gun, laying it on his desk.

At the revelation of the gun, Sonya took a deep breath. It was time to pull off the kid gloves. She had one trick up her sleeve, but if it didn't work, she'd have to hightail it out of Ryan Houseman's office and pray she didn't get a visit from Sheriff Walker tonight.

"Poppy misses you and she wants to see you one last time. She loves you and she said to say 'Monkey Face' so you would believe me."

As she said it, she leaned back in her seat with raised

eyebrows. All her hopes depended on that endearment hitting the mark. It had been a fib, of course, because Poppy never had told her, but the pet name had been mentioned twice, once by Mr. Pepper and once during the séance. Sonya kept her fingers crossed.

Ryan stood up out of his seat and bellowed, "How in the hell, did you get that...that...name!"

In an effort to stay calm in the face of the blast, Sonya responded in a firm tone. "I didn't. It was what the spirit whispered to Mr. Pepper on the morning it woke him. A terrible row ensued immediately after because Mr. Pepper's wife was horribly annoyed that Poppy was...well," Sonya tried her best to not make Poppy look like a tart, "confused about where she was and with whom. Poppy, herself, called for 'monkey face' during the séance along with your name, so if you're Ryan 'monkey face' Houseman, I have the right person."

Still on his feet, Ryan prowled like an angry lion back and forth behind his desk shooting rather hostile looks in Sonya's direction. "Ma'am, no one, and I do mean no one, knew that name. Did Pepper's wife call him that?"

"Absolutely not," Sonya replied. "Mr. Pepper hates monkeys."

Resuming his seat, Ryan glared at her from across his desk. "Are you telling me Poppy is dead."

"I'm so sorry to have to tell you this, Ryan. Poppy is dead," Sonya said softly, but then quickly added, "Only in the physical sense is she gone. Her spirit is very much alive."

No one spoke. On the highway outside Houseman's Tractor Inc., cars and semi-trucks made a lonely whooshing sound as they passed. For what seemed like an eternity to Sonya, she waited to see if he would listen. Ryan finally let out a sigh.

"If she's dead, it's almost a relief. I'm not saying I believe you," he threw his hands up in the air in a gesture of incredulity at the insanity of the situation, "and I happen to hate monkeys, too. Poppy loved them, so I let her call me that."

Here was her break.

"Ryan, Poppy came to my spirit intervention session…"

"Your what?" Ryan asked, his expression perplexed.

Sonya sighed, her attempt at another good catch phrase dashed. "Séance," she corrected. "Poppy came to my séance last night, and she told us her name and where she died."

The man behind his desk put his head in his hands.

"She really is dead. God! I want to believe you, Mrs. Caruthers, if for no other reason than I feel like a man who's been haunted. I loved Poppy and no other woman has ever come close to her."

For a minute, he sat and stared at a three-inch stainless steel man balancing on a miniature pedestal and holding a barbell. Ryan reached over and gave the tiny statue a gentle flick. He and Sonya both watched as the stick-man rocked back and forth on his pointy, metal feet.

"I'm ready to put down this weight," he said finally with a hint of exhaustion in his tone. "Where do we find her?"

Sonya sat up briskly and smiled. "If you come to my house tomorrow at around seven in the evening, I will hopefully be able to bring Poppy to us. She may be difficult because my...helper who works with me and relates well with ghosts, I mean spirits, is out of town at the moment."

Ryan squinted his eyes and answered her with an expression of uncertainty. "Well, I'll come by, but I've got one question. If she's dead, then someone had to murder her, right?"

This might be the reason Zeb didn't want Ryan to be told, Sonya suddenly realized. Her shortsightedness with the living was always a problem for Sonya.

"Well," she said drawing out the word, "that's yet to be seen. Sheriff Walker is doing some investigation regarding the Turner house being burned down and the body found in the pit. There was talk of a treasure, so maybe that brought Poppy back as well."

Ryan calmed down and again ran his hand through his hair.

"If she was murdered, I'll kill him."

"Who?" she asked tremulously.

"Rick. He killed her. I can feel it."

"Poppy fell down a set of stairs, and someone did bury her, Ryan; but that doesn't mean we have proof of a murder. Don't point blame yet. We need facts, and in this case, we actually have a chance at getting some proof with the help of the victim. If she was murdered, and you create a big hullabaloo that tips off the guilty person, we will lose our chance at resolving this completely. You need to be discrete, okay?"

Their eyes met and Ryan, after a few sticky seconds, nodded his agreement.

"She was a beautiful person. I loved her the minute I laid eyes on her. Every day since she was taken from me, I've missed her, and I'm angry, I guess. I can't get over the anger of it. I knew Ricky was lying when he said she ran off with some guy in Springville."

He sat down again like all the air had been deflated from his earlier puffed up torment.

Sonya nodded. "I do understand, and you need to know that she can't go to her next home until you let go and are at peace, too. That's why you both need to say goodbye. Ryan, if you love her, you've got to let go. If you don't, Poppy will suffer in ways no mortal can ever understand."

There might have been a tear in Ryan Houseman's eye, but he blinked and made a pretense at rubbing his temple effectually obliterating any trace of the tear's existence.

"If it's her, I'll know." He paused and went on. "I love her. I miss her, but I want her to be happy and maybe, who knows, we'll be together again someday."

Sonya smiled and stood up to go. "That," she said with finality, "goes without a doubt."

Chapter 23

"It's Poppy?" Ricky asked with a look of fear blanching his face and causing his upper lip to break out in a dewy, nervous sweat.

Sheriff Walker was enjoying himself. The morning had started out with a perusal of the forensic report from Pineville and the dental records retrieved by Deputy Kirchner from Dr. Dempster's office. It was by special request and police escort that Ricky Mitchell had been transported to the police department to discuss his wife's disappearance.

Zeb watched the human heap sitting opposite him. Ricky didn't look like a murderer, but most people are excellent at hiding their inner demons.

"We are, of course, waiting on DNA confirmation, Ricky, but the dental records match exactly. You've got some explaining to do. If you want an attorney present, you may request one. It's important, though, that at this point in the investigation, you tell us everything that happened the night Poppy died."

"I didn't kill her, if that's what you're asking!" Ricky cried throwing his hands up in a gesture of despair. "Okay, I lied about her coming back to town and I forged the divorce document, but that was because she disappeared, and I wanted to marry Melanie."

Ricky laid his head down on the wooden table between him and Zeb and moaned causing the rickety thing to wobble and shake. Zeb rolled his eyes heavenward. The cowardice nearly oozed from the pathetic man's pores. Something didn't fit.

"A jury might think that's the very reason you killed her. You wanted to be rid of her and you wanted her money," Zeb said trying to push another button.

"Money! *She* never had a penny," Ricky said practically spitting the last word with disgust. "Old Mother Turner took every dime with her when she left. I'd asked Poppy for a divorce and we'd both agreed on it. She knew about Melanie, and I knew about Ryan. We were both sick of each other and our marriage."

"When was the last time you saw Poppy?" Zeb asked.

Ricky took a drink of the bottle of water in front of him and swallowed hard.

"It was a year ago at the end of August. Remember we had the huge flood? She'd come home from being with Ryan and found me upstairs packing. Poppy was fine with me leaving. She even told me to come back for my other things anytime."

"So, what happened? Did you leave? Take up housekeeping with Melanie and never see Poppy again?" Zeb asked with a touch of sarcasm in his voice.

"It was when I went back to the house about two days later to get more stuff that I realized something wasn't right. The door wasn't locked and the cats came running and mewing like they were hungry. I called out for her, but she was nowhere to be found."

"Did you look for her in town? Ask people if they'd seen her? Why didn't you contact the police about the situation?"

Ricky rubbed his hands together nervously. Zeb saw his uncertainty about something.

"Rick, it's going to come out anyway, so you might as well tell me now and maybe I can help you."

After a short time, he seemed to make up his mind. "Melanie said we should stay quiet about Poppy disappearing. She said since we weren't divorced, I had the right to sell the contents." He shrugged. "So we did, and when people gave me the eye and asked about where Poppy got off to, I made up the story about Poppy running off with some guy in another town."

"Ryan Houseman didn't believe you, did he?"

Ricky's face puckered up like he smelled something bad. "That son-of-a-…"

"Now, Ricky," Zeb said holding up his hand, "let's keep it real. I know what happened between you and Ryan. I was there to pull him off you. He claimed you killed her."

"Houseman had the gall to attack me that day in front of the grocery store. He's crazy. If that body you claim *is* Poppy, why don't you have Houseman in here questioning him? I didn't murder Poppy. I didn't need to."

Zeb considered Ricky's claim and asked, "Why haven't you ever sold the Turner place? It's worth a fortune."

"It's not mine to sell. The house and land belong to Nellie Turner and her descendants. Can't be touched, and I found that out *after* I married Poppy and Mother Turner made sure to remind me of it daily."

"Why didn't you divorce before?"

Ricky didn't answer, but Zeb could guess the answer. It was for the hope of money. There was one last question he wanted to ask.

"Did you decide not to have children?"

Now it was Ricky's turn to roll his eyes to heaven. He shook his head.

"She never got pregnant. I lost interest in her."

"I can't hold you for murder, Rick. Someone buried your wife not more than three miles from the home you both shared for six years. You gained a modicum amount of money from her disappearance and you've forged legal documents. It's this last bit that may buy you some time in jail. I've pulled the divorce document you forged. It's six months past the date Poppy went missing. I suggest you get an attorney."

Zeb got up and signaled for one of his deputies to come and collect Ricky. He'd probably get Melanie to put up bail and the wheels of justice would begin to grind.

Once Ricky was gone from the room, Zeb collected his files and headed to his office. He believed Ricky Mitchell was innocent of the murder, but he definitely knew more than he was letting on. People who were guilty had different body language and something about the way he answered the questions made Zeb suspect he didn't do it.

Picking up his phone, he dialed Ryan Houseman's number. It was time to bring him in and talk, but, as he was dialing the number to the tractor supply, he put the phone back down on its cradle.

"Hey! Kirchner! Come in here!" he called.

"Yeah, what's up, sir?" Tommy appeared in the doorway.

"Let's take a drive and bring your new dog. We're going out to the Turner place. I'd like to see something and I might need another hand."

"Sure. I'm ready when you are," Tommy said with an easy-going smile.

Soon, they were heading out of town down along the river not far from where it had all begun. It was a nice day. Not too muggy yet, and, with the windows down, the air whipped through the car's interior bringing that scent of earth, water, and fresh-cut grass into the cab.

"Do you think Mitchell killed his wife?" Tommy asked as he maneuvered the car along the bends in the road.

"If I had one guess, I'd say no. I don't want to think Ryan Houseman did it either. If Ricky did kill her, it wasn't for the right to sell a few trinkets and to be with Melanie. I don't think he's telling the truth about the night he left Poppy. As for Ryan, if he had a motive for murdering her, it hasn't come to light. The day I pulled him off Ricky, Ryan Houseman was a crazed animal. He had blood in his eye and he would have killed Mitchell if I hadn't been there."

Tommy shook his head slightly. "What about Melanie Mitchell? How does she play into this whole story?"

"That's a good question. She certainly didn't gain much by Poppy's death unless you figure on Ricky being a prize."

Both men smiled at the idea.

"Do you think the house burning down has anything to do with all of this?" Tommy asked.

"Deputy, that question smells like you've been talking with Mrs. Caruthers," Zeb said with a hint of teasing in his voice. "Has our resident spiritualist made a believer of you yet?"

Tommy grinned and eyed the sheriff. "Actually, sir, yes to both questions. I'm telling you, she definitely has some kind of special ability. She told me I'd have two new people come into my life and it happened."

"You're not considering that dog in the back are you?" Zeb asked.

Looking in his rear view mirror at Sheba with her head hanging out the side window, Tommy said, "Mrs. Caruthers told me two new souls would come into my life, both from difficult situations. You've got to admit, Sheba's situations was pretty harsh."

Zeb considered his deputy for a moment. "It was probably a coincidence, Tom. As for your question about the Turner house burning down, that's why we're going out there. The fire chief told me it looked like the fire started in a kerosene heater in the living room. Could have been tramps staying there and accidentally caught the place on fire, but I'd like to see for myself."

"Local kids like to hang out in there, too."

"Yeah, but I want to see if there's been any digging around or signs of people looking for something. People have talked for years about a treasure out there. Poppy Turner may have been killed for it and who knows, the house may have been burned for it as well."

Scene Break

Having left Willard at Marnie's to play with Lewis and Clark, Sonya was busily unpacking her picnic basket and blanket. A cold bottle of ginger ale, crackers with cheese, homemade potato salad, and two fried chicken legs wrapped in tin foil were perfect for a springtime picnic. She'd come out to the Turner house ruins to find Poppy, who'd never returned after Fritz ran her off the day before. After talking with Fritz last night, Sonya knew she needed to find the lost ghost and bring her back fast. Chances were good that Poppy had gone home again.

The weather-beaten barn was a charming sight in the mid-day light. Painted the traditional red, it was set back far enough from the main house that it wasn't affected by the fire. A mound of hay filled its upper story loft doors and birds flew in and out making nests for their chicks high up in the old rafters.

Sonya surveyed the area to decide on a good place to lay her blanket and have lunch. There was a nice backyard in between the house and the barn where a few rickety chairs still sat. A healthy lawn stretched out in all directions, and along its perimeter were wild rose bushes, a few bright forsythias still radiant with their yellow blooms, and huge pink azaleas that were well over fifty years old. Two ancient oak trees provided a nice dappling shade, keeping the sun from being too pervasively hot.

Thinking there couldn't be a prettier place to spend a morning, Sonya put the basket on the ground and laid out her lunch. Two crows flew over and landed on the top of the barn to survey her work. She watched them as they cocked their heads to one side and strutted along the roof's edge. As if sure of Sonya's decision to stay, they announced her arrival to the rest of the barnyard denizens by making three loud cawing noises and flapping their wings.

"Oh hush! Do you really think that's necessary?" she called up to them. "Everyone is completely aware of my presence."

With the crows silenced, Sonya lay back on her blanket to gaze into the leafy canopy of the oak tree boughs above her. A soft breeze played among the dancing branches while sunlight dappled down upon where Sonya lay. Feeling drowsy, she shut her eyes to quietly enjoy the serenity of the place. The crows cawed and took flight from the barn's roof as a shadow moved between Sonya and the sunlight.

Her eyes fluttered open to see a human silhouette standing over her. Blinking, she sat up trying to make the person come into view better.

A woman's voice said, "Are you comfortable? This isn't your typical picnic spot, lady."

Pulling herself upright, Sonya realized she was being addressed by a woman who was probably in her late sixties wearing work overalls and a hat that read 'Clyde's Backhoe Service.' Grey hair was fluffed out around the cap's bottom, and on her feet were men's work boots.

Sonya offered an answer. "I'm Sonya Caruthers. I live in Willow Valley. Who are you?"

"Maybe I'm not interested in giving out my personal information as quick as you like to do," said the woman suspiciously. She pursed her mouth together and with a steely stare inspected Sonya from head to toe.

"Well…" Sonya attempted another route to an introduction, "this is the Turner farm, as you may already know, and I'm curious about the family who used to live here. Do you happen to know them?"

The newcomer nodded grudgingly. "I might and I might not. Who are you and what do ya want? People don't come out here unless they are up to no good. What's your story?"

Sonya thought it couldn't hurt to tell the truth. After all, maybe this tough-talking, ninety-eight pound (from the looks of her) character would know something.

"What I say may be a bit disconcerting for you, but I'm here about a ghost. It's a woman, and I've already spoken with her and she wants help crossing over. I believe she was murdered and she wants a proper burial."

Most people upon hearing a few statements such as those strung together would have either run Sonya off, backed away with a weak smile on their face, or declared her to be another looney in a world which had too many already. But Nellie Turner squinted her eyes at Sonya like she was trying to figure out what commune she'd wandered away from.

When she did finally speak, her tone was firm.

"What the h-e–double-l are you talking about, woman? There's no ghost living here, and this is my farm, so maybe you'd better be getting along. Take your fancy basket and put your back end on that red motorized bicycle you arrived on and hightail it back to Willow Valley with the rest of those free-love, organic food-eating hippies."

Sonya ignored the rant and honed in on the one thing the woman had said that was a clue to her identity. "This is your farm? Are you a Turner?"

Nellie Turner's jaw was set in a hard forward manner as if she hadn't any intention of acknowledging who she was to anyone, especially a trespasser. As for Sonya, she wasn't easily swayed from her intentions either. She climbed to her own two feet to be on equal footing with the tough-talking matriarch.

"If you're Mrs. Turner, I think we need to talk. I won't pretend to imagine what a difficult situation you've returned to."

The woman flicked a cursory glance over Sonya's basket of food. Taking a long shot, Sonya asked kindly, "I'm not a free-love hippy, but I did pack more food than I can eat. Would you care to have some lunch with me? We could get to know each other a bit? I don't bite and the ability to talk with ghosts wasn't a choice, it was more like being born with blue eyes or attached earlobes. It's what I was dealt by nature."

This had the desired effect. Hunger may have been a deciding factor in the decision, too, but you work with what you have. Sticking out her hand to shake Sonya's in the way of a rough greeting, the tough customer bought

Sonya's offer of lunch, saying, "Better to not look a gift horse in the face. Thank you, I would. I'm fairly famished. Been out here two days and didn't bring enough groceries. Once I show my face in Willow Valley, it'll be a full-on inquisition. I am Nellie Turner, Poppy's mama."

Chapter 24

Sonya's heart dropped at the name. The full impact of what Nellie must be feeling hit her hard. Motioning for the older woman to have a seat, Sonya's mind grappled with how to tell Nellie about her daughter's death as gently as possible. Once the food was distributed and Nellie had eaten well of the provisions, the two sat quietly after some initial exchanges of personal information.

"Nellie," Sonya said reaching out to lay her hand on the other woman's hand, "I am sorry to have to be the one to tell you something."

The older woman nodded her head and wrinkled up her nose. She blinked hard and wiped away the tears that manifested quickly in the soft pale eyes.

"I know. I think I've known all along. You spoke of a ghost. It must be my Poppy."

It was all that was said for a couple of minutes. Sonya knew how to give space to people when they needed it. After a few sips of ginger ale, Nellie cleared her throat and spoke her mind.

"Poppy wasn't an easy child by any means. It was as if the good Lord, when he divided the two girls into twins, gave one a good dose of common sense and the other little or none. Poppy was smart as a whip in school, but when it came to men, her need for acceptance and attention was a curse. It might be because her Papa died when the girls were thirteen. Rose turned inward and Poppy went looking for attention."

Nellie shook her head and looked heavenward.

"That day she brought Rick Mitchell home having already married him, I sat down and cried. I knew what he was and why he'd married her. His own papa worked in the riverboat casinos as a card shark and his mama left when the boy was two. His grandmother raised him and she wasn't up to the task being nearly sixty-five when she got him. Ricky Mitchell was running cons by the time he was twelve, and he'd grabbed Poppy on the rebound from Ryan."

"What happened between Ryan and Poppy?" Sonya asked.

"She loved him in a terrible way, and he walked on cloud nine whenever she smiled at him. That was a true love match if ever there was one. They should have married, but the truth of it was that Kathy Berkowitz, Ryan's old girlfriend, had gotten pregnant back when they were dating. Her parents sent her off to Texas to live with her aunt till the baby was born and she didn't tell Ryan about the baby. Her parents didn't want her to deal with the slap to her reputation."

"What did Ryan do?"

"Kathy was gone for a year. By the time she came back, Ryan was with Poppy. Kathy's heart was broken. She went back to Texas to live and didn't tell Ryan about the pregnancy for over two years. Then when her parents didn't have any control anymore, Kathy told Ryan about the little boy. Once Ryan found out, he of course told Poppy. For some reason, I never understood why, Poppy broke it off with Ryan and a year later married that human parasite, Ricky. She thought Ryan should go to Texas and be close to the child. It was a terrible situation."

"Did Ryan take care of the baby?"

"Ryan's father told him he should marry Kathy. He tried to do the right thing, but to Kathy's credit, she said she didn't want him to marry her unless he loved her. Besides, she'd met this new boy and wanted to marry him. As for the child, the last I heard, Ryan was trying to be a long-distance father to him."

"It's so sad. All those young lives torn apart," Sonya mused softly. "How did the marriage between Poppy and Ricky go?"

"After they were married, my days were numbered living here and watching Poppy grow miserable in her choice of husbands. I begged her to leave him, but it was as if she was punishing herself in some horrible way by staying with the no-account loser. I couldn't take it anymore, so one day, I told her I was going to live with Rose in Australia. Rosie had a baby and wanted me to come help, so I went. Never expected to stay so long, but that's another story."

"How did Poppy take it?"

"The day I told her about Rosie being pregnant and how I wanted her and me to go to visit in Australia, Poppy sat down and cried. It broke my heart. I knew how much she wanted a baby and that worthless…" Nellie shook her head and tears welled up again in her eyes.

"Anyway," she continued, "Poppy told me she wanted to leave Ricky. He would give her the divorce if she signed over half of the farm."

"Were you willing to let him have it?"

"No. The farm is in an estate. My husband, before he died, settled it on me to hold for the two girls. Rose had a right to half of it. The last thing I was going to do was to hand half of that property over to Ricky Mitchell. I told Poppy if she wanted to leave him I'd pay for an attorney and they'd have to come to some form of a settlement."

"Do you know what happened once you left for Australia?"

"Poppy wrote regularly after that and she stayed with him. Middle of last year, the letters stopped. I tried to get ahold of her. I called people I knew and finally called Ryan. He told me she'd left town and he blamed Ricky. Ryan looked for her and couldn't find her. I told Rose something was wrong, but out of the blue, I received a letter from Poppy."

"What did it say?"

"Poppy said she'd left Ricky for a man named Charlie Watkins. They were living in Springville and she was happy. She sent me a picture of herself laughing and sitting in a restaurant booth. The letter said she'd be in touch once they were more settled and her job was secure. I didn't hear from her again. I started calling people in Willow Valley and no one knew anything except that Ricky had remarried.

No one had seen Poppy in quite some time. I even called the police in Springville and told them the situation. They said I needed to talk with her ex-husband. That's when I broke down and called Ricky."

Sonya guessed how that went. "Was he helpful?"

"Told me he had no idea where she was, but that she'd signed the divorce papers and that was all he cared about and hung up on me. I was in an awful state. It had been a half year since Poppy's last letter and I couldn't get any real help over here. My daughter, Rose, was struggling with her own health issues since the birth of her baby, and I couldn't leave her. It wasn't until last month that I was able to set a date for return. All this time I've known somewhere deep inside me that Poppy was dead. It didn't come as much of a surprise when you talked about the ghost of a woman. In a way, it's a relief."

Nellie broke down again and cried for some time. Sonya held her and offered soft words of understanding. Once the sobs slowed and Nellie could drink some more ginger ale, Sonya thought it was time to push a little further.

"Nellie, you need to understand that Poppy's body is dead but not her spirit. I think she was killed and it had to be her body they found a couple of days ago in the ground at The Whispering Pines RV Park. I saw her hovering above the open pit and I've talked with her. She remembers being pushed down a flight of stairs here at this house, but before you begin to blame Ricky, you need to know she has total recall of him leaving the house minutes before she was pushed."

Nellie took one of Sonya's cloth napkins from the picnic basket and covered her face while soft sobs shook her frame. After her tears were spent, Nellie looked up at Sonya and said with a thin smile, "I'm glad to know, but I wish to God I'd seen her one last time."

As if on cue, a soft whisper of wind lifted the hair on Nellie's face. Sonya knew Poppy was there.

"It's okay, Poppy. Your mama wants to see you. Show yourself," she said gently.

The look on Nellie's face was almost one of pained hope. Her gaze darted from one vantage point to the next with an eager intensity. Poppy materialized in front of them the same way light sparkles across the surface of a lake. Suddenly, she was there with joy radiating on her face for her mother to see. Nellie reached for her, but there was nothing substantial to hold.

"Baby," Nellie almost groaned. "Oh, my sweet girl, I've missed you so much! Mama is so sorry I ever left, Poppy."

Poppy came to her and for a long minute, they stared at each other with loving smiles.

"Mama," Poppy said. "I love you, and I don't blame you for leaving. I need to be buried properly and I want to see Ryan."

Nellie nodded with a rapt expression that combined both love and grief. "I will do it, darling. Poppy, please tell me who…" she balked at the word but pushed through, "killed you."

"I don't know, Mama. I never saw them. I can't stay much longer, but you need to know one more thing."

"What? What, darling? Tell me. Please don't go," Nellie pleaded.

"The baby...I was going to have a baby, Mama. Tell Ryan it was his."

And as she said the last words, Poppy disappeared, leaving Nellie and Sonya to stare in silent horror at the vacant spot where she'd once stood.

Chapter 25

"Poppy! Poppy, come back, please," Sonya called out in hopes of bringing the ghost back to them, if only for a few seconds longer.

No reply came back to the two living women left sitting in the peaceful backyard of the old Turner house.

"A baby," Nellie said more to herself than to Sonya. "Poppy was pregnant."

Sonya sat down again on one of the old metal chairs as the growl of a car's engine came up the road. Both women stood up quickly and went to see who was pulling up into the drive. Upon seeing it was a police car with Zeb and Tommy in the front seat, Sonya felt a sense of relief. She got up from the blanket and walked down to meet them.

"Sheriff, I think there is someone here you'll want to meet."

They all three turned their gaze toward the top of the drive. Nellie walked around the corner of the remains of the house and made her way to where they stood.

"Guess I'd better introduce myself," she said shakily. "I'm Nellie Turner, Poppy and Rose's mother. I think I need to sit down."

Sonya saw it coming and Zeb moved with a quickness

that came from his years of working in law enforcement. Nellie's knees were buckling, but he got to her before she went down. The shock of everything she'd heard and experienced had caught up with her.

"Let's get her to the clinic. She's as white as a sheet," he said calmly. With an almost effortless act of male strength, Zeb lifted Nellie up off her feet and carried her like a cradled child. He put her in the backseat of the police car and signaled for Tommy to hit the lights not the siren.

"Mrs. Caruthers, do you want to ride with us to the clinic?" he asked.

Sonya was kind of rattled herself, but she pulled herself together quickly and answered him.

"No, I have my moped. I'll follow you."

In less than thirty seconds, the police vehicle disappeared from view. Sonya found it hard to actually move. The experience had exhausted her, too.

"Sunny," a soft voice said close behind her.

Sonya smiled. Taking a deep, cleansing breath, she let it out.

"Is that you, Fritz?" she asked with hope in her voice.

"Of course, it is. Do you think I'd let my favorite lass be alone when she needs me most?"

"It's been a hard day, Fritz," she said, her voice thick with the emotion of everything she'd been through and heard. "I need you to tell Poppy to come with us. She needs to stay at our house. I think we're closer to learning who killed her. Tell her we will bring Ryan to her."

Sonya didn't hear from Fritz for about ten minutes, but

he came close to her again and said, "Come on, my girl. It's taken care of and she's with us. I will ride on the back with Poppy. I'll stay with you the whole way."

It was the right thing to say and Fritz was as good as his word. He was the faithful friend, a protective spirit and the supportive presence Sonya needed. Love is that way. Even when we can't see it, it's there.

Scene Break

That evening, Sonya coerced Nellie into staying with her at her home. She put her to bed after a long, warm soak in the tub and a heavy dinner of homemade sourdough rolls and chicken soup. The exhausted Nellie was asleep before her head hit the soft pillow.

"I think she needed some mothering herself," Sonya said to Willard as they both descended the stairs into the living room. "Poor Nellie has been through the mill, as they say. Let's not wake her till mid-morning and no barking at the kid on the skateboard tomorrow, Willard. Okay?"

Willard tilted his head to the side as if trying to make out Sonya's strange language. Fortunately, dogs have a brilliant ability to know what we mean before we even say it, so he gave her a two-paw high-five on her knee and trotted off in the direction of his food bowl.

"Good, we're set for our visit with Ryan tonight, and if I'm not mistaken, Zeb Walker will probably show up, as well."

The time they'd spent at the clinic with Nellie had

given Sonya ample time to talk with Zeb about everything she'd learned, but instead of discussing it there, she thought it would be better if both Ryan and Zeb talked with Poppy themselves.

Fritz had spent the last two hours babysitting their ghost visitor and making sure she didn't wander off. Finally, he'd figured out a way to manage her. Once Nellie was in bed and asleep, Fritz took Poppy into Nellie's room and tucked her into bed beside her mother. With a warning not to touch the woman, Fritz was certain the ghost would stay put and went down to sit with Sonya.

"I'm absolutely exhausted," he fussed from the top of the kitchen table. "Some of the dead can be as annoying as most of the living."

Sonya burst out laughing at Fritz's truism. She shook her head and lay down the wooden spoon she was using to mix a cherry dump cake.

"I love you, Fritz! You are such a darling person. Some of the things you say give me such a chuckle."

Fritz, for his part, was delighted to hear Sonya's admission of affection. He sat up straight on the table and reveled in his ladylove's pleasure at his witticisms.

"I must tell you, Sonya, my sweet, the sea hag of Dunbar wasn't willing to let me take up residence again alongside my living kin at the castle. Mary MacGregor Dunbar is a mighty foe and if she'd been born a man, I'm sure she'd have routed the English from the land of the Scots with only her tongue as a weapon."

"Sounds like you weren't as charming as you needed to

188

be to win her back," Sonya said dumping the ingredients into a baking pan.

Fritz sighed. "I spent a lifetime with the woman, and I don't want to spend my afterlife with her, too. As for her, I think she's taken up with one of those roaming soldiers from the Culloden battle. She told me I can visit once a month and to stay away from our great-great-great-grandson who's turning my home into a flop house for whiskey poachers."

Sonya couldn't help it; she laughed again and turned to put the pan into the oven to bake. She gave the unfortunate Fritz an understanding, loving smile.

"It's the way it goes, poor Fritz. Nothing stays the way we most want to remember it. In your heart, you're upset at Mary moving on. But remember this Fritz, if you'll continue to go over to visit your family, on her terms, of course, you'll see how hard they're trying to save the ancestral seat. Mary may come around, and, if so, you may have a better relationship with her than you did while you were alive."

Though Fritz was refusing to even semi-materialize, the tabletop wobbled with his fidgeting. After a few minutes, he appeared to have thought it over and the table was quiet.

"Sunny!" he said brightly with a renewed vigor in his tone. "I'm going to do it, but first, I'm going to run that interloper from my land."

"Fritz!" Sonya called to the retreating Laird. "Wait! I've got two questions before you disappear."

There was a hovering in the atmosphere of the kitchen.

"Yes, my dear?" Fritz answered.

"Did you make sure Poppy is going to stay?"

"She's upstairs with her mother and content at the moment. No promises."

"Last question, does the interloper have a name?"

Fritz's voice boomed, making Sonya jump. "Yes! Mary's taken up with a damnable MacDonald! The clan that's been trying for three hundred years to make Dunbar land their own! I will na have it!"

The atmosphere of the room cracked and snapped with Fritz's departure. With her shoulders a bit hunched at the loudness and ferocity of his exit, Sonya stayed still until she was sure nothing was going to be sucked up into the energy vacuum.

"Whew! I wouldn't want to be one of those poor MacDonald's," she said out loud. Thinking it over for a second, she said, "Oh, they'll probably love it, especially Mary. She might give Fritz another chance if she sees how jealous he is."

Sonya's musing on Fritz's love life was cut short by the doorbell. Sticking her head around the kitchen's doorframe to see who was there, she saw it was Ryan Houseman.

"Well, here goes. Let's hope Poppy doesn't do a runner."

Sonya went to the door and opened it.

"Come in Ryan," she said with a smile. The words had no sooner left her lips than a great rush of air smelling of gardenias and a ferocious outburst of the word "Ryan!" came full speed down the living room stairs, through the hall and burst over the two living people still standing in the doorway like a summer thunderstorm.

Chapter 26

"What's going on?" Ryan yelled as both he and Sonya's hair lifted from the turbulent air swirling around them. "I feel like something is kissing my face!"

Sonya's hair and the scarf around her neck were beating time with the personal tornado taking place on her front porch.

"Come inside! And for goodness sake, Poppy, BEHAVE!" she shouted.

A car door slammed in front of Sonya's house, and, as she pushed Ryan in through the screen door, she saw Zeb Walker and the skateboard boy on the sidewalk in front of her house. They were both standing with their mouths completely dropped-jawed and their eyes looking at the whirlwind happening only on Sonya's porch.

Willard came bolting out of the door barking and hopping about as the whirlwind whipped the hanging flower baskets about and threw seat cushions from the wicker chairs out onto the lawn. Upon seeing the skateboard boy, he growled menacingly and tore off the porch toward the kid. The boy actually screamed, causing Zeb to jump and jerk back as the teenager ran down the sidewalk yelling, "MOM!"

"Please," Sonya called down to Zeb, "get inside before the entire neighborhood thinks it's Armageddon!"

Zeb quickly scanned the street, opened the gate and ran up the front porch steps. Once he was inside, Sonya slammed the door behind him. She turned around to find Ryan, with a sickly, white face, sitting on the sofa, while a groggy Nellie stood in a bathrobe watching her should-be son-in-law fend off the ardent kisses of her ghost child.

"Poppy!" Sonya yelled at the top of her lungs. "You've got to calm down! You're scaring Ryan and your mother, not to mention the sheriff!"

Poppy was obviously thrilled to have her beloved once again within her grasp. It took some time, but she slowed her affectionate embraces and her chilly kisses to one or two every five minutes.

Everyone found a seat in the living room and Sonya brought out hot tea to drink.

"Have you got anything stronger in there, Mrs. Caruthers?" Zeb asked. "I don't think tea's going to cut it after…" He paused to watch Ryan's hair ruff up and slick back down on its own, "what we've seen and been through."

Sonya nodded mutely, and, being shaken up herself by the sheer intensity of the whole experience, she thought maybe a drop or two of whiskey in their cups would do the trick. As she grabbed the bottle from the liquor cabinet in her dining room, Nellie called out, "Hold the tea, Sonya, and bring me a stiff glass of Bourbon."

Once everyone had a few sips of their refreshment of

choice, Sonya decided it was time to get Poppy to tell her story and help her to cross over.

"Okay," she said, "Poppy, you've got to settle down and pull your energy together so we can hear what you want to say to both your mother and to Ryan."

For a few minutes, nothing happened. Nellie, Ryan, Zeb, and Sonya sat quietly, but the intensity and the anticipation that filled the room were palpably felt by all.

"I was pushed down the stairs, but I don't think I died till after the miscarriage. I don't know who did it."

Female sobbing sounds immediately moved about the living room. Ryan's face looked like someone had punched him, and Nellie sat in her chair in tears again. This was when Sonya was truly able to use her gift to help the distressed people on both sides of the physical plane of life.

"Poppy," she said firmly, but with compassion, "stop your crying. What's done is done and your baby is in Heaven where you need to be soon. Tell those you love what you need to say and I'll help you go to your child who's waiting for you."

The crying stopped abruptly. It was as if Sonya's words reminded Poppy of the reality of her motherhood. Yes, maybe the baby had passed over, but it still existed and it might need her.

"Ryan, I love you, and I've been searching for you for such a long time. Ricky told me he would only let me leave him if I told him where the treasure was. I told him it didn't exist. He got in his car and left. That's when I fell."

Ryan sat motionless and put his head down in his hands

and cried. "I'm so sorry, Poppy." His words were choked with emotion. "I love you, and I always will. God! If I'd known you were pregnant, I'd have never been able to go on. If I ever get my hands on the person who did this, I'll... I'll kill them."

The air became static-filled and Sonya knew that Poppy was upset.

"No! Ryan, don't do anything like that, please. I want you to go on and live your life without any more regrets. Find someone. That's why I needed to talk with you. It's time to let go...for both of us."

Nellie stood up and went over to Ryan, putting her arms around him. She'd had only a little time to come to some understanding of her own loss, but she understood his grief. Ryan gave her a weak smile.

"Poppy," she said firmly, "your mama loves you, sweetheart. Ryan's going to be fine and he needs to go on with his life. I'll take care of him, but you need to go on to God and your baby. We'll make sure your remains are treated with respect. I love you. I love you so much, baby."

The air became still, but Sonya knew Poppy wasn't gone, only resting.

"I'd like everyone to send her a farewell and ask for her to be taken by those good spirits who have been waiting for a long time to bring her home," Sonya asked the group.

Even Zeb lowered his head and, along with the other three in the room, they wished her well. Soon, a loud crack split the air of the room in two. A feeling like they'd all been simultaneously zapped by electricity made them jump in their separate seats. Poppy was gone. As Sonya felt the remains of the ghost's departing surge gently through the room, she knew Poppy's passing was the kind all of us hope for--a happy, peaceful one.

Scene Break

The four people stayed quiet for a few minutes after Poppy departed. Zeb asked Sonya to come into the kitchen to talk, so Nellie and Ryan would have some time.

"What just happened in there?" he asked, his manner awkward and unsure.

Sonya saw the liquid in his glass shake from his reaction to Poppy's passing.

"I've been doing this for years and, quite honestly, what happened with Poppy was extremely unusual. Most ghosts who've died under difficult circumstances are so weakened that they don't have much power to communicate. Poppy's energy was amplified by her desperation."

Zeb shook his head and sat his glass on the kitchen counter. "Mrs. Caruthers, I don't usually share information with anyone outside my office, but we do have dental records matching the body from the pit. It's Poppy, but I'm no closer to learning who killed her."

"You gained some information tonight that you didn't have before, Sheriff. Poppy was pregnant, and, if you ask me, someone else knew, too. Maybe that's why the Turner house was burned down. It is possible someone knew Nellie Turner was coming home and was going to move

Heaven and Hell to find out who killed her daughter. I don't know much about forensics, but if there was any residue from that miscarriage in the house, that's why it was burned."

"Who could have known about Nellie coming home?" Zeb asked.

"I think we need to ask her because that's definitely a lead in this investigation."

Zeb laughed and picked up his glass, tipping it in a toasting gesture toward Sonya. "You want a job working for me, Mrs. Caruthers? I could use you in all my investigations."

"Anytime you want some help, Sheriff, you know where to find me."

"Call me Zeb, would you?" he asked with gentle earnestness.

"Um," came a man's voice from the doorway between the kitchen and the dining room. "Nellie and I would like to thank you, Mrs. Caruthers. Before I go home, could we talk," he looked at Zeb, "about how we can find the murderer?"

"Absolutely," Sonya said. She'd taken the cake from the hot oven and put it on a wire rack to cool. "But before we do anything, we're going to have something to eat. Best way to deal with shock, cherry dump cake."

Sonya smiled up at them both as she got some plates ready.

"Something smells wonderful," Nellie said, coming around the corner into the kitchen. She sat down and gave the other three a sweet smile. "Thank you, Sonya. Knowing my Poppy is at peace and in a wonderful place is a relief. No mother wants to live the life I have these last six months."

"Grieving takes time," Sonya said, bringing the cake to the table and putting it down in front of Nellie. "A piece of cherry dump cake and a hot cup of tea can take the edge off of it, but it's not an answer. We need closure."

Nellie looked at the cake as it sat with steam gently escaping its crumbly, delicious topping. "This isn't your first rodeo, is it, Caruthers?"

"No, and it probably won't be my last. After these kinds of experiences, I've found that people need something comforting. Warm food, soft beds, and caring people will usually do the trick."

They all sat around the kitchen table and talked about their memories of Poppy. There was some laughing and a few tears, but for the most part, they celebrated her life with good cheer. After the stories were exhausted, Zeb got around to asking some more pointed questions.

"Ryan, on the night Poppy died, were you together?" he asked.

"Yes, we'd been to Pineville to eat dinner. I'd asked her to leave Ricky and she'd agreed to talk with him that night. She wanted out of the marriage but was afraid he'd try and take her family's land."

Nellie turned to Zeb and asked, "Sheriff, do you think Ricky had someone kill her?"

Zeb put his fork down neatly across the plate and

thought for a second before answering.

"Something in my gut says it wasn't Rick. He can be a low-life, but I don't get the feeling he has her death on his hands. Knowing that Poppy was pregnant doesn't change things much. Rick wanted to be with Melanie, but having a baby doesn't mean people stay together anymore. Nellie, is there any truth to the stories about a Turner Treasure?"

"No, well, not to my knowledge. That was an old tale. For some reason, people believed the Turner farm was taken over during the Civil War by bushwhackers, who had gotten ahold of gold bullion meant for the armory in St. Louis. Neither Herman, my late husband, nor his parents ever gave any credence to that story."

"Well, I can't see someone killing Poppy for it, so it had to be for another reason. Ryan, do you stay in touch with Kathy Berkowitz?"

Ryan had a mouth full of dump cake, but he swallowed hard and answered.

"Yeah, I see Kathy a lot. She has our boy, Parker. Kathy lives in Springville and I visit every week to pick up Parker and bring him home for the weekends. Why?"

"Kathy may have been jealous of your relationship with Poppy. You shared a child and maybe she didn't want you to be with Poppy."

"I don't think Kathy killed anyone," Ryan said, his tone a bit defensive. "I've had to catch mice in live traps and let them go in the woods for her. She's never talked about me and Poppy. There wasn't any point."

Zeb got up and went to fetch the coffee pot. Everyone

had moved on to beverages with less spirit to them.

"If someone wanted Poppy dead, it has to be for either: money, love, or revenge. Those are the top three reasons. What we need is a way to flush the killer out. Nellie, did you tell anyone you were coming back to Willow Valley? It's too coincidental that your home burns down a few days before you are due to arrive."

"I did tell Bertha Edmonds but swore her to secrecy. She was related to my husband, Herman. They were cousins on his mother's side and she lives in Pineville. I wanted to have someone here in case I needed help."

Zeb jumped on this bit of information.

"Did you talk with her about helping you find Poppy?"

"I told her I hadn't heard from Poppy and I was worried. She was upset, too, about the situation and said if I needed anything, to call. I've been on the phone once a week with that ninny of a sheriff in Springville about Poppy. He tells me every time that they've got no record of a Poppy Mitchell living in Springville."

"Nellie, why didn't you ever reach out to our police department in the last six months about Poppy?" Zeb asked.

"I did!" Nellie said putting her glass down on the table with firmness. "I talked with old Sheriff Dalby. He told me he'd check into it for me. I've never heard back from him. I called two months ago and they told me he'd passed away."

Zeb shut his eyes and leaned back in his chair. Sonya noticed what a handsome face he had. He let out a sigh and answered Nellie.

"Yeah, we let Harry Dalby stay on and help out, but he

was not doing so well those last few months. He kept forgetting things. I'm so very, very sorry, Nellie."

Sonya took a sip of her coffee and put down the cup.

"Let's go back to how someone might have known about Nellie coming home. It is probable that Bertha spoke to someone about Nellie's return and that she'd be staying at Turner farm. I do believe whoever killed Poppy, didn't want there to be any chance that they'd left something behind at the scene of the crime. Best way to fix that is to burn the house down."

Zeb nodded. "It's possible whoever killed Poppy has moved on. We need a real clue."

The room was quiet for a long moment. Sonya sat up straight in her chair with a look of excitement on her face.

"You've got one," Sonya said forcefully. "Nellie, you've had the proof of who killed Poppy the whole time!"

Chapter 27

Everyone looked at Nellie like a bouquet of balloons had popped free from the top of her head.

"What?" Zeb asked with a voice full of incredulity. "What have you got Nellie that you haven't told us about?" Zeb asked.

"Heck if I know!" Nellie exclaimed. "Ask her!" She pointed to Sonya.

All heads swiveled in Sonya's direction.

"The letter, Nellie...Please tell me you brought the letter that was sent to you supposedly by Poppy when she ran off to Springville with the imaginary lover."

No one moved. It was like they'd all been frozen in their chairs.

"You've got a letter, Nellie?" Zeb asked.

Nellie nodded. "I do, but not here. I left it with my things out at the farm. If you'll go get it, Sheriff, I'll be glad to hand it over to you."

"Holy, moly! That's got to have DNA from the killer on it," Zeb said as he got up to go.

"I'm going out to the farm. Ryan, you want to come?"

"I do."

"Wait!" Sonya said, making them stop and turn around.

"If you get the letter, please, Sheriff, don't tell anyone you have it. It might come in handy to keep that secret to ourselves."

Zeb nodded but teased her a little bit. "Mrs. Caruthers, you telling me how to do my job? I hope you're not getting any funny ideas about how to manage this investigation."

Sonya didn't answer but gave him an innocent, sweet smile. Zeb grimaced and left with Ryan in tow. The two women returned to the living room.

"I'm glad they're gone. Sonya, I've got an idea about how to bring the killer out of the woodwork," Nellie said.

"When they have the letter, Nellie, they can check suspects against the forensics retrieved from it. The sheriff will have much more to go on then."

"Nah, that's going to take too long. I want justice in *my* lifetime."

Sonya considered her point. "What's your idea?"

"What if we let it be publicly known that the body found at The Whispering Pines RV Park was, indeed, my Poppy. People already suspect it anyway. You and I should go to Tilly's Cafe and talk about the letter. We'll say how with DNA testing, the letter I have will lead the police to the identity of the killer."

"Nellie, you can't do that. It's the shortest way to your own cemetery plot," Sonya said forcefully. "The letter is the perfect bait, though. We need to find a better way than putting a bullseye on your forehead."

"I'm going to do it!" Nellie said putting her hand down

with a smack on the chair's wooden arm. "And I'll tell people I'm staying out at the farm in the barn. That will let everyone know I'm home and alone. I'll need backup. Will you help me?"

Sonya didn't like it. If the killer was still around Willow Valley or the surrounding area, they wouldn't want that letter to get into the hands of the police. Putting Nellie's life in danger, and her own for that matter, sounded like a terrible idea, but something occurred to her.

"Nellie, what if we did tell everyone in town. I'll get a manicure at Lana's and tell her to spread the news. We'll go to lunch at Tilly's Cafe and let the gossip boys at Table Three know about the letter and how you're going to take it to the sheriff. That will squeeze the killer out and force their hand fast. But to keep us safe, we'll set a trap for them at the barn and they'll never see us or even get near us. I do have one question for you, though."

"What?" Nellie asked, her face lit up with excitement.

"Does your barn have a root cellar?"

"It does and it's a nice one made of limestone rock. We never used it for our garden crops because we had refrigeration by then, but the kids loved to play in it."

"Do you access it through a trap door or through a ground entrance at the side of the barn?" Sonya asked.

"A side entrance…I get where you're going with this, Caruthers, and I like it. It's like a live animal trap. We entice them in with the letter and slam the door shut. Trapped like a rat!"

"Perfect analogy, Nellie. I couldn't have said it better

myself."

Scene Break

The next morning after a light breakfast, Nellie and Sonya generated their plan for bringing justice to Poppy's killer. When they called Sheriff Walker to see if he had retrieved the letter, Nellie told him her idea. After some initial yelling and explaining about due process and how he wasn't going to be held responsible for their probable deaths, he finally gave in and promised to check in on them at dinnertime.

Willow Valley was having a busy morning along Main Street. Tilly's Cafe was packed with all the locals. Lucky for Sonya and Nellie, the good weather and a special on flapjacks had encouraged a high level of patronage that day.

"Let's sit right in the middle if we can get that one," Sonya pointed to a table that was free.

They sat down and Marsha, the head waitress, walked over to take their order. Upon seeing Nellie, her progress slowed measurably as if she was trying to place the face.

"Mrs. Turner!" she exclaimed so that everyone in the cafe turned to see what Marsha was going on about. "It *is* you! My goodness, I haven't seen you since before Poppy left."

Marsha made a beeline over to Nellie and gave her a hug.

"How are you, Mrs. Turner? How's Poppy?" Marsha asked, her face full of happiness and hope. Tilly's Café's head waitress was the same age as Poppy and had gone to school with Nellie's daughters.

Nellie's heartache welled up with the remembrance of Marsha being Poppy's friend. With a trembling smile, she looked up at the still beaming Marsha and said in a voice choked with emotion, "Oh, dear, I'm so sorry to be the one to tell you, but my Poppy is dead. It's her body they found in that horrible pit out at Whispering Pines RV Park."

There was a universal sucking of air into lungs followed by a reversal of that same air in a chorus of shocked exclamations from the cafe's patrons.

"Oh, my God!" Marsha cried. She dropped her order pad on the ground. "Poppy? Dead? Who would have wanted to kill her?"

"I…I…I don't know," Nellie stammered. The actual words had reawakened the wound in Nellie's heart.

By this time, the entire cafe was hanging on Nellie and Marsha's every word. It was Earl Higginbotham, one of the Table Three coffee drinkers, who voiced what the rest of the locals were thinking.

"Do they have any idea who might have killed her, Nellie?"

Nellie looked at Sonya, who with deliberation slowly shut and opened her eyes once as a way of encouraging her.

"I've come back from living with my other daughter, Rose, in Australia, but while I was there, I received a letter from Poppy saying she'd run off with some man from Springville. That was a lie because we know Poppy was already…dead."

Nellie stumbled again from the emotion. Sonya reached over and placed her hand on Nellie's giving her the courage to continue.

"Someone else wrote that letter to keep me from looking for Poppy. I've got that letter and I'm taking it to the sheriff. With that DNA testing, they'll be able to find out who killed her."

No one spoke for half a second; then everyone talked at once.

"Good! I hope they catch him and put him away forever," one coffee drinker said forcefully. The rest of his buddies all agreed with equal vehemence.

The women patrons whispered to each other and lots of heads shook back and forth at the horribleness of such a crime happening in what they thought was a safe, small town. Sonya and Nellie finally got to give their order to Marsha, who was red-eyed and constantly expressing her sympathy to Nellie for such a terrible thing having happened to poor Poppy.

Once Marsha disappeared into the kitchen, Sonya and Nellie were left to talk and sip their coffee. They didn't dare discuss the letter or Poppy again. Sonya knew it had been enough for Nellie to announce it to so many of her old friends and neighbors.

They did hope, however, that someone would ask where Nellie was staying. They didn't have to wait long because out from the back kitchen came Tilly. She walked straight toward their table, pulled out a chair and sat down with her own iconic cup of coffee. Everyone in the cafe surreptitiously watched and kept their conversations low so as to hear better from their own seats.

"Marsha told me what's happened, Nell. I'm so sorry to hear about your girl. Poppy was a sweet thing. This is going to kill Ryan Houseman. He's been carrying a torch for her since the day she left Willow Valley. Do you need a place to stay while you're here or are you staying with Mrs. Caruthers?"

Tilly gave a short, friendly nod at Sonya and waited for Nellie's answer.

Nellie patted Tilly's hand that was lying on the table and smiled.

"Thanks, Till. It's good to see you again. I'm coming to terms with all this and I'm staying out at my old place, the farm. I've made a nice little nest in the barn and I'm getting a real estate agent to come out and put the place on the market. I won't be staying long. My daughter, Rose, is still out in Australia and she needs my help."

Tilly nodded with a stern expression and lowered her voice for a more confidential exchange.

"You know, you've set yourself up mentioning that letter, Nell. You'd better hightail it over to the sheriff's office and hand that letter over as quick as possible. Your life's not worth a plug nickel until you do. The killer may still be here in town."

Nellie shot Sonya a knowing look and raised her own voice enough to let most of Table Three and a few others close by hear her reply.

"Thanks, Till. I've got to get back to the barn and collect the letter. It'll be in the sheriff's hands by tonight.

Can't go before because I'm waiting on the real estate agent this afternoon."

Tilly gave Nellie a penetrating look along with a wily grin barely tinging the corner of her mouth. She nodded with her own knowing expression saying, "Well, good, Nellie. You need anything, anything at all, just give me a call. I'm glad to see you again, and I'm sure sorry about poor Poppy."

Tilly got up and went back into the kitchen. With the bait fed into the gossip machine, all that was left was to hope it would be well strewn throughout the town. Soon, their lunch arrived and they enjoyed their fried chicken, homemade biscuits, and mashed potatoes, along with a sizable helping of green beans seasoned with onions and bacon drippings.

"Goodness!" Sonya said with gusto after having a few bites of the best fried chicken she'd ever had. "That Tilly is an amazing cook. It can take years to perfect this. Reminds me of the way my mama used to make it."

"Honey, I may have to have Rose and her Aussie hubby move back home from Melbourne," Nellie said as she chewed on a second chicken leg. "I've missed my Southern food. Have you tried your biscuit yet? Light as a dream."

Sonya laughed softly. "Good luck with getting young people away from a beach Nellie. In the meantime, should we order some of that incredible homemade banana cream pie?"

Chapter 28

Deputy Tommy Kirchner was putting Sheba, his new police dog trainee, in the back of his car when his cell phone rang. Looking at the incoming number, he realized it was Laney. His heart skipped a beat and he quickly answered it.

"Hi!" he said, the excitement in his voice extremely apparent. "What's up?"

"You've got to get over here to the office, Tommy," her voice agitated and worried sounding. "It's Ricky Mitchell and he's angry with Dr. Dempster about turning the police on to him. Doc is out, but I'm afraid for Percy. If I have to, I'll deal with Mitchell myself." In a low whisper, she said, "I think he's been drinking. Percy is trying to barricade him at the reception area, but it's getting nasty. My two cleaning appointments ran out of here terrified."

"I'll be right over," Tommy said. He heard yelling going on in the background of the call. "I'll bring the sheriff. Hold on and if it gets too ugly, you and Percy need to lock yourselves in a room."

"I'm not afraid for me, Tom. I'm afraid I'll get mad and hurt Ricky. Get over here as soon as you can."

Laney hung up and the deputy ran back inside to get Sheriff Walker. He found him sitting at his desk looking at an old letter encased in a plastic bag.

"Sheriff, there's a problem over at Dr. Dempster's office. Laney Bodwell just called and said Ricky Mitchell is there and he's drunk. She says he's mad at them for providing dental evidence against him in Poppy's murder investigation."

Zeb quickly got up from his desk. "Let's bring that nincompoop in and put him in a cell. I'm so sick and tired of him muddying the water. Come on, Kirchner. Grab a Taser. I hate to use force, but Mitchell can be a handful. He's like a slippery pig when he's fighting mad."

The two officers made what would have been a ten-minute trip, in less than five. As they pulled up in front of the dentist's office, Percy came bolting out of the front door, his facial expression one of crazed fear and his bun wobbling on the side of his head. The t-shirt he was wearing had the neck stretched over his shoulders like someone had pulled it down forcefully halfway to his elbows. With both upper arms restrained tightly by the shirt, Percy ran at the police vehicle waving his hands frantically at Tommy and Zeb.

"Come on, let's save Percy," Zeb said, his tone cynical. "Rick's going to be ornery, so get that stun gun ready."

They stepped free of the vehicle and that's when they heard the gunshot. The two men exchanged thunderstruck expressions, while Percy let loose a high-pitched scream and went running off down the side alley of the dental office.

"Get around to the back. If Rick tries to escape that way, I want you to hit him with Taser," Zeb said. "I'm going in the front."

Tommy didn't argue. His training taught him to follow orders. He followed the retreating figure of Percy while Zeb strode up to the office's front door and pushed it open. There quivering in a corner was Ricky and standing over him with a shotgun was Laney. She smiled broadly at the sheriff.

"There's one hell of a hole in the ceiling tiles over the reception area, but Ricky's being a real good boy now, aren't you, Rick?" she asked while tapping the barrel of the gun with a nicely manicured fingernail.

"Oh yes, I'm all done, Laney," he stammered. "I'm awful sorry to have bothered you. I'll go with Zeb."

"You got a license for that gun?" Zeb asked Laney, hoping she did.

"I have my conceal carry and my paperwork on the gun. If you need to look at it, it's in my purse. Give me a minute and I'll get it for you."

Zeb gave a congenial nod as Tommy burst in through the back door.

"Better go tell, Deputy Kirchner you're okay," he said with a grin.

Laney walked off toward the back with the shotgun's barrel dropped down next to her right leg and Zeb gestured in a bored, distasteful manner for Ricky to get out of his corner. Dr. Dempster walked in through the front door and spied Zeb, Ricky and the gaping hole in his ceiling.

"Tell me Laney didn't shoot Percy," he said turning to Zeb. "They've been fussing at each other all day over who's going to pull all the back-dated files and scan them into the computer."

Zeb pointed at Ricky saying, "Laney's been teaching Ricky, here, to not drink and harass his local dental practice."

This appeared to agree with Dr. D. and he nodded sagely in agreement with his office manager's proper use of a firearm.

"Well, I'll have to replace those tiles. Looks like she deliberately used one shell. That'll make it easier. Hope there isn't any damage to the roof." He studied the ceiling with a critical eye. "Ricky, I ought to have you pay for this. Laney's not the kind to use her gun unless she feels it's a worthy cause. You must have been kicking up a lot of dust in here."

"He ran off two clients and roughed up Percy," Laney said coming back up to the front with Tommy, who had a huge grin on his face. "Percy's extremely upset and that makes my blood boil, Ricky. No one picks on Percy," Laney said with a look on her face that made Ricky cringe next to Zeb.

"I…I'm sorry," he said shaking his head and slurring his words, "I got to drinking and the more I thought about everything, the angrier I got. You're trying to prove I killed my wife, Doc."

"Ricky, where I'm taking you, you'll get to sober up and make amends by doing some community time. I think Judge Winston will be glad to let you come over and fix Dr. D.'s ceiling and maybe do some work on his roof as well."

Zeb had to help Ricky out the door, and upon getting into the back seat of the police vehicle, he saw his old dog. "Hey, this is *my* dog," he said. Sheba, not holding any grudge for the terrible neglect she experienced at his hands, sat serenely on her side of the seat.

"*Was* your dog," Tommy said, sliding into the car's front passenger side. "We're teaching Sheba to search for illegal drugs, bring down attackers, and track missing people." He gave Ricky a steely look. "And deal with pain-in-the-ass drunks."

"Which brings up an interesting point," Zeb added as he maneuvered the car out into afternoon traffic. "We may have a break in Poppy's murder investigation. Nellie Turner is back and she brought a letter with her that was sent, most likely, by either the murderer or their accomplice. Should take us right to the killer."

Zeb, using the rear view mirror, looked in the back. At first, Ricky said nothing in return. He lifted his gaze and staring Zeb right in the eyes, said, "Well, I wish you luck, Sheriff. Poppy's killer is probably on the other side of the country by now. I know I would be, if I'd murdered someone. But I didn't, so I don't have anything to worry about."

Ricky turned and fixed his gaze on the scenery passing by out his side window. The rest of the ride to the police office was quiet, but everyone had a great deal on their mind.

Scene Break

As Sonya's Morris Minor chugged up the dirt road to the Turner farm, the afternoon was coming to a close. A balmy seventy-degree temperature was going to make for a perfect evening free of humidity. Anyone in Missouri will tell you the blight of summer humidity is one of the reasons for the state being sometimes called Misery by its tongue-in-cheek native population.

Sonya parked the car. She rarely drove the Morris, so if their visitor tonight saw it, hopefully, he would believe it was Nellie's and that she was home. Taking their things up into the hayloft, they made a comfortable spot to sit where they'd be unseen. Sonya had packed a thermos of coffee to keep them awake, plenty of snacks, two flashlights, and the always necessary can of bug spray. Those same natives will also tell you that ticks, fleas, and mosquitos are the other three reasons Missouri gets the Misery nickname.

The root cellar was in fairly good shape and its entrance was easy to see from the loft above. Someone thirty years ago had run electricity to it, so there was a single light bulb hanging from a metal fixture, and, after a light cleaning, the phony accommodation wasn't too disreputable.

"Do you think anyone will believe I'm staying in this place?" Nellie asked as she hit the dust accumulated on her overalls sending it billowing up into brown clouds around her.

Sonya continued to knock down cobwebs in the rafters. "No worries. We're going to make it look hospitable enough and with some music playing on a radio inside, it'll give the illusion of being inhabited."

They dragged the two metal garden chairs from the backyard into the cellar and arranged them around an old dairy can with a square piece of plywood for a top to make a makeshift table. With hay strewn over three wooden pallets laid end to end, Nellie added her bedroll to give the impression that this was where she'd been living.

"Let's put my picnic basket on one of the chairs. The food poking out over the edge will make someone think you're here. Also, we need your luggage bags laid on top of the bedroll and completely opened," Sonya directed.

Once the stage was set, they turned their attention to making sure their surprise prison would be able to perform its job. The root cellar door was substantial enough to hold anyone locked inside. It was made of oak and it had two iron L-brackets mounted to either side of the opening. A two-by-six plank of wood, on its own metal hinge, rotated and dropped into the brackets securing the door completely.

"That should do it," Nellie said. "I'm going to put some papers on the table and you tie the rope to the end of the plank. Then, all we need to do is wait."

Soon they were nestled in the loft, hoping the killer would take the bait they'd thrown around at Tilly's and Lana's earlier that day. They weren't roughing it too terribly. Fortunately, neither woman was skittish about vermin. Spiders, on the other hand, had caused some difficulties, but most of them had been run off with the broom.

"I hope Zeb didn't tell anyone he had the letter. That'll ruin it for us," Nellie said watching the sun beginning to set over the old oaks in the yard. "I used to miss this place sometimes, but now it will always be the place where my child died. I wish I'd been the one to burn it down."

Sonya breathed deeply and watched the crimson and purple streaks in the summer evening sky darken, creating a once-in-a-lifetime painting that would never be seen again, even if the world existed into eternity.

"Poppy's in a wonderful place, Nellie. Any suffering she may have known is over for her. You've got some time ahead of you for the grieving, but not forever. If there is anything this crazy world teaches us, it's that nothing lasts forever, even loss."

Birds flew among the trees, telling each other of the possible threat sitting in the barn loft. Sonya and Nellie enjoyed the bird's winged acrobatic show with a dusky sunset for a backdrop. A motorized vehicle of some sort murmured in the distance. It was coming up the road in the direction of the farm.

"Oh, my God!" Nellie whispered. "This could be it."

Chapter 29

"I'll get the rope ready for the lock. You be ready to slam the door. Don't forget to hide in the stable area," Sonya said breathlessly.

They were both actually terrified at the realization their plan might be falling into place. In minutes, they'd be face to face with a killer. Nellie scrambled down the loft ladder and tucked herself into a stable stall right behind the root cellar door. Sonya worked the rope mechanism to make sure it would swing the two-by-six easily and without hiccups into the metal brackets. Both women heard the crunching of tires on gravel and the sound of an engine as it whined to a stop in the driveway in front of the burnt-out house.

"Hello!" called a woman's voice. "Hey! Is anyone here?"

Neither Sonya nor Nellie dared to speak. They crouched down further into their different hiding spots.

"Mrs. Turner! It's me, Marsha! I wanted to come out and bring you some dinner!"

"Was it Marsha who killed Poppy? But why?" Sonya thought frantically to herself. Feeling a brush of wind against her cheek and a low whisper in her ear, she knew

Fritz was back.

"Fritz!" she whispered. "Tell me that's you?"

"Yes, my love," came the tender reply.

"This is not the time for that. I'm trying to catch a murderer. You should go home."

"Ah, come on, Sunny. Let me help. I've had a killer day and I need some fun."

Sonya peeked over the edge of the loft's window to see if Marsha was still standing down there.

"Interesting choice of words, but if you're staying, maybe we can use your help," she whispered. "Please go down to where that woman is standing and chase her into the root cellar below. Okay?"

"Chasing women was a specialty of mine two hundred years ago," Fritz said softly in her ear.

"And that's why your wife is still mad at you two hundred years later. Go!"

In less than three seconds, a shrill scream was heard from Marsha. Her hair was being whipped into a frenzy of movement like invisible bats were attacking her head. She took off running toward the barn like a mad woman. As Fritz chased her into the cellar singing a dirty ditty about a Scottish sailor's wife, Nellie slammed the door and Sonya flipped the locking plank into place.

"Mrs. Turner! Are you here?" Marsha sobbed loudly.

"The letter is already with the sheriff, Marsha. If you've come out here to get it, I don't have it!" Nellie yelled through the door.

"The what? I don't know what you're talking about, Mrs. Turner. Tilly sent me out here with a basket full of food. What letter are you talking about?"

Sonya and Nellie, standing by the door, exchanged 'oops' expressions.

"I don't think she's the one. Should we let her out?" Nellie said in a whisper.

"Yeah, and maybe give her an apology, too."

They started to lift the plank from the locking brackets but Sonya stopped.

"It may be a lie. Let me call Tilly and make sure," she said to Nellie.

"Okay, Marsha. We're calling Tilly first," Sonya yelled through the planks.

After a long wait on the line, Nellie got it straight from Tilly's mouth that she had indeed sent Marsha out with a care basket. It had some of her own carrot cake she'd made that morning. She hoped Nellie enjoyed it. After she hung up, they opened the door for Marsha.

"What is going on out here?" Marsha said, her hair still a fright and her face smudged with dirt.

"Come up to the loft Marsha," Sonya said, leading the way. "We can't take any chances the real killer might show up."

"The what?" Marsha blurted. "Are you two crazy?" She looked around wildly.

"Now, slow down, girl," Nellie said patting the frazzled Marsha on the shoulder. "We're trying to bring the murderer of my Poppy to justice. It was sweet of you to come all this way. We didn't mean anything by hustling you into the root cellar, well, other than we thought you were a cold-blooded killer."

Marsha stood stock still with a mystified expression on her face.

"How did you get that weird song to play in my ear and the air to rush around me? Have you got special wind machines and stuff?" she asked looking around.

Sonya threw out a plausible answer.

"You must have heard the radio playing and it's been a breezy day, Marsha. I think it all came together and you were probably a bit nervous being out here on your own."

Her expression showed she wasn't exactly convinced. Reaching up to touch her frazzled head of hair, she said, "Well, I'd like to stay, Mrs. Turner. Poppy was a friend of mine, and if you think the killer might come out here tonight, I'd like to be in on catching him."

Sonya and Nellie nodded.

"Honey, do you mind waiting to leave? The killer could be out there waiting. It's better if you stay with us for a little while," Nellie said in a motherly tone to Marsha.

"Besides, we could use a younger set of legs to climb down that ladder. Marsha, better go move your car. It's recognizable. Pull it around behind the barn on the left side. It should be well hidden over there. When you're done, climb back up here and be ready to wait. You'll need to turn your cell phone to silent," Sonya instructed.

Once they were all back in position up in the loft, the sun sat completely. Bats took the place of the birds in the sky, feeding on the flying nocturnal insects.

"I hear a car coming," Marsha said softly.

No headlights broke through the darkness.

"I've got a feeling this is our man," Nellie said.

They strained their ears to hear the approaching vehicle, but soon, even the sound of the engine was gone.

"Let's get into position," Sonya said in a whisper. "Whoever it is doesn't want to be seen or heard. I'm pretty sure, this time, we won't be making a mistake."

Marsha went first down the ladder and helped Nellie in the darkness. Everything in the cellar was ready. They both hid behind the stall divider while Sonya sat ready for the slam of the cellar door below. For the last hour, Fritz had been silent.

"I'll go out and see who it is, if you want, Sunny." he said softly in her ear.

"Stay close by Fritz. I may need your help here. Suddenly, I'm terribly nervous," she replied.

The full, bright moon cast a lovely light over the tranquil farm. From Sonya's vantage point, she saw a figure moving along the edge of the road. It stayed in the shadows of the trees and along the fence until the darkness of the oak trees obscured its advance from view. Sonya's heart was beating in her throat. The silent figure certainly didn't want to be seen or heard. By staying on the grass, their footfalls made no sound.

Sonya strained her ears for any signs of someone being in the barn. Nothing other than the ceaseless chirping of crickets, June bugs, and the nighttime breeze could be heard. For five minutes, she sat hoping for the cellar door to slam shut, and that's when she smelled it—smoke! Something was burning.

"Come on, lass," Fritz said beside her. "You've gotta get down from here. Go!"

"Is it the barn? I can't, Fritz!" Sonya answered. "What if the killer is down there?"

"Go down Sonya! I'll handle him," Fritz commanded.

The smoke was filling the barn as Sonya descended the ladder. Once on the ground level, the black thickness in the air made it impossible to see.

"Nellie! Marsha! Where are you?" she called. Choking from inhaling the smoke, she turned to run outside but stopped upon hearing voices calling to her from inside the cellar.

"Fritz!" she screamed. "They're in the cellar! You've got to get them out! I can't breathe anymore."

The wooden plank latch swung up and the door was thrust open. Nellie and Marsha pushed through the cloud of smoke. All three women quickly ran out into the yard and breathed deeply. Birds flew from the barn's loft over their heads, and vermin came scuttling out, running past their feet.

"What happened? How did you get locked inside?" Sonya asked between coughing fits.

Nellie was trying to suck air into her lungs. She was bent over at the waist resting her hands on her knees and intermittently coughing, as well. Instead of answering, she shook her head. Marsha had gone to the far end of the yard and sat down on the ground. She, too, was trying to inhale fresh air.

The fire within the barn grew and roared as it consumed the hay, the ancient timbers, and the dry wooden exterior. Things exploded inside and the sound of rafters falling and crashing in upon each other could be heard.

"I didn't see the face," Nellie finally answered. "It was my fault. I couldn't hear anything, so I peeked around the post and ran smack dab into this person all in black. Whoever it was had a gun and motioned for me to go inside the cellar. Their head was covered with a ski mask. Marsha followed like a lamb. The person grabbed my knapsack with the papers and left."

"They tried to get rid of the evidence," Sonya said ruefully. "They've got to be gone."

"Not quite," came Fritz's voice from behind Sonya, making them all jump. Sonya whirled around and saw two people walking up the road. The closer they got, she realized one of them was Zeb Walker, the other...

"Melanie Mitchell? Well if that doesn't beat all!" Marsha exclaimed.

Chapter 30

"She tried to kill us!" Sonya declared pointing at Melanie. "Where's the knapsack? That'll prove it was her!"

"I don't know what you're talking about," Ricky's wife hissed back. "I came out here because Ricky said to come talk with Mrs. Turner about Poppy."

Nellie walked over to Melanie. "You're a liar and that ring on your finger proves it." Nellie pointed to a beautiful blue sapphire on Melanie's left hand.

"This ring was given to me by Ricky," Melanie stung back. "It's my wedding ring."

"That's my Poppy's ring. You were the one who pushed her down the steps and look, Sheriff, Melanie's left-handed, right?" Nellie demanded.

Melanie wouldn't answer.

"When you pulled the gun on us, I saw that ring in the light. No doubt about it, you were the one who made us go in and lit the fire to finish us off."

"It was her," Fritz said in Sonya's ear. "She's got dark spots around her. She has the mark, Sunny."

The blood in Sonya's veins slowed. People who had amassed black spots, dark holes pulling on what goodness there was left in a person, were frightening to meet. If

Melanie had more than one, she'd done some pretty bad, soul-damning deeds.

"You've got to tell the truth about Poppy," Sonya commanded, looking straight at Melanie. "You've got to make amends, Mrs. Mitchell, if you killed her. This is more important for you than for any other person standing in this circle."

Something in Sonya's tone momentarily cooled Melanie's hostility. The sneer on her face froze for a minute and, in her eyes, Sonya saw doubt.

"The black spots around her have begun to writhe and pulsate," Fritz whispered. "Gross things, evil things."

Sonya saw the doubt leave Melanie's eyes and a coldness return.

"I haven't done anything, and you've got no proof other than this lunatic," she pointed at Nellie, "claiming that I pushed her into that cellar."

Everyone was quiet, so when Marsha spoke, her soft words were heard perfectly.

"No one has mentioned the cellar. How would you have known anything about it, if you hadn't been there."

Melanie went for Marsha with both hands. Her face twisted with rage. Zeb pulled her back and put handcuffs on her.

"Might as well be a family reunion tonight at the police station, Melanie. I've already got Ricky doing time, but nothing like what you're going to do. We'll find the knapsack. She's pitched it somewhere. It's a matter of time and a good dog's nose. Funny, but now we have a dog that can do that for us."

As he walked her back down the dirt road, sirens climbed up the highway meaning the flames must have been seen or Zeb had reported it. The fire trucks were on their way. Sonya, Nellie, and Marsha turned around to watch the Turner barn collapse in upon itself.

"This finishes it," Nellie said. "That ring on Melanie's hand was my mother's. I'd given it to Poppy and she always wore it. That filthy piece of human waste must have taken it off my baby's hand. I'm telling you, Ricky Mitchell had a hand in this, too. There's no way one lone woman lifted a body, got it into a car and dug a hole three miles away to bury it. Let's go to the police station. I want what's mine."

As the fire continued to burn and the fire trucks descended on the farm, Sonya and Nellie dropped Marsha back at her car. With gratitude for friendship in times you least expect it, they thanked her with hugs and promises to come by Tilly's later.

"Why do you think they killed Poppy?" Nellie asked softly as they drove back to Willow Valley.

"I can't answer that, Nellie, but rest assured. You're about to find out."

Scene Break

It was a wild scene in the police station when Sonya and Nellie arrived in the reception area. Melanie was being fingerprinted, and she was yelling for her right to a lawyer.

Sheriff Walker had her handcuffed to a chair taking samples for a ballistics test from her hands.

"Mrs. Mitchell," Zeb was saying, "we need to take these samples and your fingerprints. Your husband has already admitted burying Poppy's body. Once we find the knapsack, it'll have your fingerprints on it. You're about to be put away for murder and for attempted murder."

"That's a dirty lie! He tossed her down the stairs because she'd gone off and gotten pregnant by that two-timing Ryan Houseman!"

As Sonya was turning around to say to Nellie that maybe they should come back later, Nellie was already moving in Melanie's direction like a bulldog about to attack.

"Nellie! Don't do it!" Sonya said, but it was of no use because Nellie already had Melanie by the hair.

"Give me my mother's ring you ripped from my child's hand before her body was cold!" Nellie growled. She grabbed Melanie's hand, pulled the ring free from her finger, and slapped Melanie across the face before Zeb pulled her off of his prisoner.

"Never again," Nellie said with so much menace in her voice that Melanie actually cringed backward from her, "will you wear what rightfully belonged to my daughter. This ring," she showed it to Melanie, "is going to be destroyed with a hammer into a thousand little bits for having been on your filthy finger."

No one spoke. Melanie and Nellie's gaze locked. One woman with fear on her face, the other, with pain and contempt.

"Nellie, you need to back off," Zeb said, "or I'll have to lock you up, too, for battery. Go sit down over there. Ricky has given a complete confession about Poppy's death. Once I have Melanie in her cell, I'll come back and explain everything."

Thirty minutes later, Sonya and Nellie were sitting in a bleak conference room when Zeb walked in and sat down. He gave the two women a weak smile.

"Melanie won't admit anything, but what we have from Ricky matches what we know. After Ricky left the night of Poppy's death, he went to Melanie's house, but she wasn't there. Her mother told him she'd gone to find him at the Turner farm. He went back and found Poppy at the bottom of the stairs dead. She had bled from the head and he saw she'd miscarried. He was horrified and he panicked."

"So, he didn't kill her," Sonya murmured. "Poppy didn't think so either."

Zeb continued. "Well, he found Melanie that night at a favorite bar they liked to go to and told her that Poppy had fallen down the stairs. He said Melanie told him he was better off telling everyone she'd run off with some man so that he could sell everything off. When he told her he didn't have any rights to the house or land because it was in an estate, he said she told him with the right documentation, he could have half the farm."

"So when did he figure it out that Melanie had killed her?" Nellie asked Zeb.

"According to him, he took the ring off Poppy's hand

and gave it to Melanie. That year, the river flooded down by The Whispering Pines RV Park. Where Marnie was building her pool, there was a boggy area beginning to dry out. He didn't have to dig much to bury Poppy. Later, when word got out that you were coming home from Australia, Melanie must have gotten worried about you asking for a real investigation into Poppy's death. Any forensic team worth their salt would have found the residue of the blood at the bottom of the stairs. That's when he finally knew it had been her because the night your house burned, Ricky said she came home smelling of kerosene. She took a bath and had difficulty getting the stink off her."

"So, did he ask her about it?"

"Yes. She wouldn't admit to it, but he said he knew because Melanie told him it was lucky it had burned. No one would ever find the evidence of Poppy's blood or miscarriage. That cinched it. He'd never discussed the miscarriage with Melanie. She'd refused the night he buried the body to go with him. The only way she'd have known about it was if she'd been there when Poppy died."

Nellie burst into tears. "Oh, Zeb, promise me she'll never hurt anyone ever again. Promise me she'll be locked up."

Zeb reached across the table and took Nellie's hand.

"I promise, Nell. Melanie Mitchell will go to prison and stay there."

"Why did she want Poppy dead?" Sonya asked. "Was it in hopes of selling the farm for the money?"

Zeb shook his head in a gesture of mystification.

"Ricky says he believes Melanie was jealous of Poppy, but I think it was greed. He says she's been on him since their marriage to find a way to sell off the land and the house. It was worth a fortune, and she knew it. He said it never would sink in that even with Poppy's death, hc couldn't get the rights to the estate. I think if you and Rose had been living here, Nell, Melanie would have probably come after you, too, and in the end, she did."

Removing his hand, he leaned back in his chair and studied the two women. "There's one more thing. Chief Robertson has called me about the fire. Your barn is gone."

He paused and added, "But they found something interesting buried below the barn's foundation. It was a natural cave that had been blocked up, probably used to hide things. The falling timbers of the fire broke through the brick floor of the barn, opening it up."

Sonya and Nellie waited.

"They found a cache of Civil War gold ingots, Nellie. Interestingly enough, the marks are CSA, or Confederate States of America. I think you're an extremely wealthy woman."

"They found gold?" was all Nellie was able to say.

"The treasure was real, and it's been down there for a hundred and fifty years. Good thing it was buried in the barn. If it had been in the floor of the house, Ricky and Melanie probably wouldn't be around to stand trial for murder."

Nellie was quiet for a few minutes. Then with slow, deliberate words, she said, "I'm going to take that money and build a nature center. There's over a hundred acres of unspoiled natural beauty out there and I'll have a memorial to Poppy and her baby right in the middle. Too much sadness and horror have taken place there. Making it a place for people to go and enjoy its pastures, old trees and quiet, will wash away the dark deeds and bring a bit of peace to anyone who needs it."

Chapter 31

Getting Nellie ready to go home to Australia had been a challenge. They'd spent the week since the murder of Poppy had been solved, buying out different stores for things that, according to Nellie, were difficult to buy in the land down under.

Melanie Mitchell's DNA was found on the letter she'd sent to Nellie about Poppy and her fingerprints were found on the retrieved knapsack. After the forensic proof was put in front of her, she admitted her guilt and asked for forgiveness. She actually was glad to come clean. The day she left for sentencing in Pineville, Melanie never looked back.

So with a bit of sadness at losing a good, new friend, Sonya drove Nellie to the airport for her flight home and helped get her luggage through the airport check-in. It had been a struggle managing the four heavy suitcases, but Nellie was delighted to have so many things to take back to her family.

As she was ready to go through the gate, she handed Sonya an envelope.

"I've got something for you. It's just a way of saying thank you for helping me and Poppy. Once the nature center is done, I'll be back to put Poppy's ashes inside the memorial. For now, they're resting at the Willow Valley Cemetery. I hope you'll be able to come to the consecration."

"Of course, I'll be there. Would you like me to open this while you're here?" Sonya held up the card.

"Oh, please wait till I'm gone, will you?" Nellie asked. "It'll make me feel better if you open it once I've gone through the gate."

Sonya nodded and gave the dear friend a tight hug.

"Have a safe trip and you've got my email address, so let's stay in touch. Okay?" Sonya asked.

"Will do."

Nellie picked up her purse and walked through the gate. The two women gave each other one more bright, happy, smile and waved goodbye. Once Nellie was enveloped by the crowd, Sonya looked down at the envelope. She pulled it open and pulled out a card. Flipping it open, to her utter shock she saw inside a check for fifty thousand dollars. Sonya, for at least ten seconds, stood in one place staring down at the numbers. After counting the zero's twice, she looked up and discarding her usual restraint yelled as loud as she could, "THANK YOU, NELLIE TURNER!"

Out of the sea of heads and barely audible over the ocean of voices, Sonya heard, "YOU'RE WELCOME, SONYA CARUTHERS!"

There was nothing left to do but go home and put on her dancing shoes. She had a date to keep at the farewell party for Mr. Pepper at his lodge that night. As Sonya walked out of the airport's main entrance with a bounce in her step, she thought about Fritz and Eloise. Would they be good and not cause a scene at the dance?

In the end, they were both perfect ghostly guests at the farewell party, and to their credit, even did the jitterbug together on the lodge's piano, always a favorite place for dancing, especially for those who have the courage to give it a try.

Thanks for reading!

Made in the USA
Coppell, TX
27 June 2020